WOLFPACK

Written By
Eric S. Brown

MoonDream
PRESS
AN IMPRINT OF COPPER DOG PUBLISHING, LLC

Moondream Press
An Imprint of Copper Dog Publishing LLC
537 Leader Circle
Louisville, CO 80027
www.copperdogpublishing.com

Ordering Information:
Special discounts are available on quantity purchases by corporations, associations, and others. For details, contact the publisher at the address above.
Printed in the United States of America

Credits:
Author: Eric S. Brown
Managing Editor: Michael H. Hanson
Creative Director: Helen H. Harrison

ISBN:
Trade Paperback: 978-1-943690-22-0
Kindle: 978-1-943690-23-7

Library of Congress Control Number: 2018933834

Fiction: Horror

CONTENTS

DEDICATION

This book is dedicated to
Lyle Blackburn and Ghoultown for their
awesome music,
my family for their constant support,
the creators of Jonah Hex for the
inspiration,
and horror western fans everywhere.
—*Eric*

INTRODUCTION

by James Robert Smith

SOME WRITERS HAVE THEIR FINGERS ON THE PULSE of America's readers. You know those folk—they strike with their books seemingly at just the right moment to ride the cresting wave to commercial success. The first with a certain kind of romance. The one out of the gates with a vampire novel. The guy with a feel-good yarn to beat the ages.

Sometimes it seems as if Eric S. Brown has a similar talent. His books sell great and his name is everywhere when you're searching for action and adventure fiction. For a while—and this was before I met Eric via the Internet—I would wonder how he could see the wave coming in time to toss his board on the salty brine and ride it to shore.

But you know what?

That's not it. That's not it, at all.

Eric doesn't catch the wave.

His bleeding *makes* the wave.

I won't say Eric was doing zombie novels before anyone else. That wouldn't be true. But he was doing his kind of zombie novel before the rest. It wasn't his fault that every wannabe zombie writer started aping his work. He made it seem easy and different, and so a host of followers got in line behind him and made it look like he was the first.

And who was writing flesh-eating Sasquatch books before *Bigfoot Wars* exploded onto the scene? (I could say I was, but *The Clan* won't be out for at least another year—victim of scheduling by my publishers at Tor/Forge Books). At any rate, Eric Brown had already conceived, written, and published a horror novel featuring gut-munching Bigfoot creatures when there wasn't another such book on the market! How long before a couple of dozen other writers are out there start aping his work? (Sorry. I had to say it.)

And now, here I get to write the foreword to *Wolfpack*. Once again, Eric has jumped in where nobody else seems to be. It's a western. Not only that, but it's a horror western. Oh. And ceasing to stop there, it's a horror western featuring werewolves. But don't look now! Not only are there werewolves, and not only are they total bad asses, but the werewolves are the anti-heroes of the book!

Yeah, that's right.

Get in line, wannabes. I know you want to try to duplicate what Eric has done here. You want to tackle a horror western presenting werewolves in the lead. But guess what? Eric got here first, and Eric has already done it better than the rest of you. But go ahead, if you want to.

The sincerest form of flattery is imitation and all that sort of thing. However, while you might copy the form, you ain't going to be able to copy the style. Nobody does this kind of thing better than Eric S. Brown.

Bank on it. I have.

PART ONE

Demon Dead

JEREMIAH LOVED HIS JOB. SURE, IT WAS DANGEROUS and a lot of folks would pause before doing it, but the way he saw it, he got paid to blow things up. What could be more fun than that? And the pay. . .only the foreman himself made more than he did. Jeremiah finished placing the dynamite in the correct spots along the rock face and ran back towards where the detonator awaited him. Claude was waiting on him there was along with a small crowd of workers eager for him to finish up so they could get back to their jobs. As soon as the smoke cleared, they would be up there in the debris with their pick axes, clearing out the area so that the track could be laid. The massive rock slab was impossible to move and far too large to bust up by manual labor in any reasonable amount of time. Or so said the railroad system investors.

"You ready?" Claude grumbled as Jeremiah reached the detonator.

"You know it, boss man." He grinned at Claude as he placed his hands on the plunger that would send the electrical impulses along the cables into the TNT. Once it was pressed: *WHAMMO*! No more rock. Jeremiah shoved the plunger toward the earth. The explosion seemed to shake the very ground beneath his feet. He watched as jagged bits of rock soared into the air.

"That'd do it," he said, turning to Claude.

"It had better," Claude warned him. "I'm behind schedule as it is. I sure don't have the time for you to calculate out and place another round."

Something stirred inside the cloud of dirt and dust where the rock had been.

"Who in the devil is that?" Claude asked.

Jeremiah shrugged. He couldn't see into the dust any better than his boss could. Squinting, he could see the outline of something that looked like a man moving about among the debris.

"You made sure the area was clear, right?" Claude challenged him.

Jeremiah flinched as if Claude had slapped him across the cheek. "Of course I did," he answered, trying to hide his anger at such an insulting question. He was a professional, not some idiot who'd just toss a lit stick of dynamite at a target and run away screaming for folks to get clear.

"Oh sweet Lord have mercy on us!" one of the nearby workers cried out. Panic erupted all around as the crowd of lookie-loos tried to scramble away from the site, shoving and pushing at one another in their desperation to get away. Jeremiah saw Claude, frozen in place, his mouth hanging open in apparent disbelief, as he stared towards where the rock had been. Slowly, Jeremiah turned his head to take a look himself. A *thing*—there was no better word for it— stood at least ten feet tall. It came swaggering out of the cloud settling dust. It had a head, two arms, and walked upright like a man but the resemblance ended there. Its very skin looked to be bleeding. Drops of red wetness rolled off its body from head to toe. Exposed, thick muscle could be seen under the light of the midday sun as it calmly strolled toward the workers.

Its sunken eyes glowed like twin orbs of blue fire above a mouth that appeared to be made of metal.

"You," the thing rasped in perfect English, pointing at Jeremiah and Claude. "You have released me. Why?" It dragged out the words in a sort of constant growl.

Jeremiah didn't have the slightest idea how to answer the thing. Claude, unbelievably, stepped forward to meet it. Despite its size, maybe Claude thought it was a man injured by the blast, or perhaps he had simply lost his marbles.

"It's okay," Claude assured the thing. "We'll get you to a doctor. We got one at the main camp. You're gonna be just fine."

Jeremiah realized with a start that all the other workers were long gone, leaving him and Claude alone with. . . whatever it was. The creature reached out with one of its massive hands, grabbing a hold of Claude, its fingers atop his skull and thumb below his chin. It squeezed until Claude's head folded up with the sound of crunching bone. Jeremiah let out a yelp of terror as Claude's blood splattered onto him. He felt his bowels release. There was nothing in the world he wanted to do more than run but he couldn't. He was too scared to move. Jeremiah stood there shaking as the creature dropped Claude's body and moved up in front of him. It bent over, a hideously long tongue flopping out from between its jaws to lick at his cheek. The tongue was cold as ice and scraped against his flesh like a piece of jagged stone, leaving small cuts and nicks in its wake.

"Do you know who I am?" The creature's booming words sounded like thunder in a darkened sky.

Jeremiah couldn't speak. He managed to shake his head in the negative. The creature reared back in laughter for what seemed like an eternity. Jeremiah's whole body was shaking with deep, primordial fear by the time the laughing subsided. The creature towered over him and Jeremiah waited to die.

"Little man," it told him, "You have loosed a plague upon your world like none you can imagine."

The creature looked away from him in the direction of the railroad crew's main camp and sniffed the air. "For now, you may live as you've brought about my freedom. Enjoy your last days as they shall be short."

It walked on towards the camp, leaving him completely alone except for Claude's corpse. As soon as the thing was out of his sight, Jeremiah slumped to his knees, weeping, tears rolling openly over his cheeks. Something deep inside of him told him that he had just murdered the world. An hour later, he was still there, his skin burning in the harsh rays of the sun, long after the distant screams from the camp had ended.

* * *

Many miles away, Sarah snapped awake. An arrow protruded from the center of her ribs, its shaft sticking upwards into the air from between her breasts. With a growl of pure fury, she ripped it loose and tossed it aside. She rolled off her back, springing to her feet. Nearby she saw Yule swinging the dead body of an Apache above his head by one of its legs. Meat and bone gave way to centrifugal force and the dead Apache's body tore free from the leg, flying like a stone from a sling into a group of Apache warriors who were charging at her giant brother. Over half a dozen arrows suddenly spotted Yule's chest and back but Yule kept right on fighting as if he didn't even notice they were there. Sarah's attention was so focused on Yule she didn't see the Apache warrior closing in on her until the Indian sank the blade of his tomahawk deep into her already-swollen left shoulder. Cursing herself for being stupid, she tore the Apache's head clean off his body with a powerful upward thrust of her right hand. The warrior's headless corpse tumbled into the grass at her feet, coming to rest on its knees like it was praying. She looked around, dazed. Something more than the arrow through her heart had knocked her from her saddle. An intense feeling of cold and evil had come over her like a tidal wave before the Apache's ambush had begun. She couldn't explain the feeling but she knew it had been real.

Sarah shelved her confused thoughts for later and drew her sword to join the battle waging around her. Graham had sent her, Yule, and Samuel ahead to lure out the Apaches' main force so that he, Shannon, and Zed could flank them, and the Family could wipe out the bulk of the marauding Indians in one engagement.

An arrow slammed into her side as she rushed forward to meet three more of the Apache. Next time, she thought, Graham could be the bloody bait. Sarah's blade took the first Apache's head, slicing cleanly through the man neck in a spray of blood. Her backswing drove her sword into the side of another's skull. The last of the three warriors stared at her wide eyed as she yanked her blade free from his companion's head and plunged it through his chest to the hilt, her face inches from his own.

"It's not nice to shoot a lady out of her saddle," she whispered as she twisted the blade of her sword around inside of him. He screamed to the sky and then went silent. She caught sight of Samuel. He'd gone wolf as his talent for magic was next to useless in such close combat.

His hybrid form, somewhere between wolf and man, towered over a startled Apache warrior that he had grasped by the shoulders. Samuel leaned forward, his jaws parting, as he bit off most of the Indian's face. The Apaches were beginning to realize their ambush hadn't been an ambush at all but rather a pre-planned trap they'd fallen for as the rest of the Family came riding up behind their ranks, guns blazing.

About time, Sarah thought as she saw Zed riding up in his saddle, both hands off the horse's reins, firing his Colts so rapidly even her enhanced senses couldn't keep track of the number of shots. The Apache dropped like flies. Next to him, Shannon swung from his horse to the ground, landing with his Winchester already braced and ready against his shoulder. The rifle spat death and he worked its lever time and time again with steady thrusts. A smoking cigar dangled between Graham's lips. He motioned for Zed to take out a fleeing Apache with one hand and dispatched another himself with the Colt he clutched in his other. The whole road and the edge of the woods around the Family were washed in blood. The bodies of the dead and the dying were scattered everywhere. Gun smoke and the stench of cordite hung in the air, burning Sarah's flaring nostrils as the battle ended as quickly as it had begun.

Graham looked her, Yule, and Samuel over then commented, "Well, that was sloppy. A few of them actually managed to get away."

Samuel reverted to human form and stormed towards her, anger in his blazing yellow eyes. "It was Sarah's fault. She froze when they hit us!"

Suddenly, Zed was between Sarah and Samuel, the palm of his hand pressed against Samuel's naked chest. "Hold on now, Sam. I ain't never in my life seen Sarah freeze up," Zed argued.

"No," Sarah admitted, "he's right, Zed. It was my fault."

Graham raised an eyebrow in shock then shrugged. "Job's done well enough. I highly doubt any of those boys that escaped will be causing trouble again anytime soon. Samuel, Yule, you two get us some proof to take to the colonel so we can get paid and let's get out of here."

"I hear that," Zed whooped. "Reckon we could all use a good drink about now."

Claws grew from the tips of Samuel's fingers. He used them to dig into the flesh of his own thigh, removing a long knife sheathed under his skin near the bone of his leg. Sarah shuddered at the sight. Samuel's magic allowed him to store weapons under his skin and she had seen him do it more and more of late but it still disgusted her every time he took one of them out. Grinning like a devil, Samuel sat about collecting the scalps of the dead Indians. Yule did so as well but without the obvious pleasure that Samuel took in the grizzly work.

"You okay?" Shannon asked her with an expression of sincere concern. "It's not like you to slip up. . .ever."

"I don't know," Sarah said. "Something happened, Shannon. It was as if I felt the whole world screaming inside my head. One second, everything was fine, the next, everything went dark and I woke up on the ground with an arrow in my heart. I wish I could really explain it but what I felt in that moment. . ."

Graham rode over to where they stood. "We can sort out what happened later," he told them, apparently having overheard their conversation. "The colonel's waiting."

* * *

The colonel glanced up from the reports and other paperwork covering the top of his desk as Graham and Samuel entered his office. Samuel wore a new set of black robes, a cowl obscuring the features of his face. The black robed figure plopped two dozen blood-encrusted scalps onto the colonel's papers. The colonel frowned at Graham. "Of all the others, did you have to bring him?"

Graham chuckled. He had brought along Samuel not only to annoy the colonel but to vividly remind the military man exactly who he was dealing with. Samuel's presence helped assure the Family would be paid in full for their services rendered and promptly if for no other reason than to get rid of them as quickly as possible.

"The Apache warriors are dead," Samuel growled and gestured at the scalps as Graham flashed the colonel a toothy smile.

The colonel opened the drawer of his desk and passed Graham a thick roll of bills. "I'll say this about you boys," the colonel nodded at Graham, "you always get the job done. Can't always count on that with most others these days."

"Mighty kind of you to say, colonel," Graham tipped his hat. "You have any more *issues* that need to be dealt with, you know how to find us."

Samuel gave the colonel a final scowl and led Graham from the office. As they walked out into the street, Graham could tell Samuel was fuming over something and wasn't about to let it slide.

"Why?" Samuel asked. "Why do we continue to deal with the humans in this manner?"

"Money!" Graham laughed as if the word answered everything.

Samuel eyed him.

"Money keeps us safe and gives us power," Graham explained. "Besides, what else are we going to do with our time? This way we can do what we do best and get paid for it to boot. Come on, Samuel, sometimes we even get to play at being heroes." Graham's grin was wide and bright.

"The humans are inferior. They are meat. Nothing more."

"Be that as it may," Graham tipped his hat at an attractive blonde woman they passed as they strolled towards the saloon, "they have their uses and I would rather be working for them than hunted by them any day."

Samuel grunted, letting Graham know their argument was far from over as they swung open the saloon's door, stepping into the cooler, semi-darkness inside.

Zed and Yule sat at the bar, two empty whiskey bottles sitting beside them as Zed poured shots from a third. Shannon and Sarah sat at a table in the rear of the saloon well away from the few other scattered patrons. He and Samuel joined them at their table.

"The colonel sure paid up fast," Shannon raised a glass at Graham. Graham noticed at once that something was still off about Sarah. Her normal stone cold confidence seemed shaken to its core.

Before Graham could say anything to her about it, she met his gaze. "What's our next job?"

"You're in a hurry to get back in the field." Graham stared her down. "You don't need to prove anything, Sarah. We all know you're the best."

"It ain't about that, Graham. I just have this feeling that we need to head west. Something's happening out there."

"West?" Shannon sat his glass aside. "We're in Texas. How much further west can we go?"

Graham and Sarah ignored him.

"What is it? How do you know we're needed there?" Graham asked.

"She's right," Samuel fessed up, stunning them both. "I feel it too. Something very old and very evil has been awakened."

"Great," Graham sighed, giving up getting a grasp on what was happening, deciding to just roll with it. "West it is then."

* * *

The town of Hamner was a quiet little place. Most of its residents were good, Christian folks to the point that Niven's saloon struggled more than other business in the town. Joe Niven couldn't bring himself to pull up roots and leave, though. Hamner had a certain charm to it. The surrounding hills were beautiful and he couldn't think of a better place to be raising Heather. His wife, Emma, had passed on when Heather was just a wee thing. The folks here had helped him so much then. . .Heather was going on sixteen now, a young woman in her own right and just as stubborn and tough as her mother had been. Niven didn't need to worry about her walking down the street alone like he would have in a big city back east or in some gold rush, boom town. In fact, if there was any kind of trouble here, she was usually the cause of it. Michael, the man who ran the town's stables, still hadn't let him forget how she had broken his son's jaw after Michael Jr. had teased her about her short hair. Three years gone by and Michael swore his son had never fully recovered, though his jaw had healed up just fine. Michael claimed the damage to his son's pride would never fully heal. A man or boy in Michael Jr.'s case didn't forget something like that. That whole mess was made worse by the fact that Heather was small and thin for a girl her age. Her temper was epic however and her spry little body was a heaping ton tougher than it appeared to be. Michael wasn't really angry at him over all of it anymore. It was more like Michael enjoyed ribbing him about how unladylike his daughter was, and whether he liked to admit it or not, it was true. Beyond her being too short for most folks' liking, Heather was a tomboy who would rather be out hunting rabbits with a rifle than braiding her hair or buying dresses. For all her hardness, even her worst critics couldn't argue that she wasn't adorable. Her hair was flaming red like her mother's had been and her eyes a deep, alluring green. The freckles that spotted her cheeks only added to her natural beauty. Troublemaker or not, Niven was proud of her. He knew no matter what she decided to do as she grew older, she would do all right. He was still rubbing away at an already clean glass, his rag squeaking against its side, as Sheriff Long entered the saloon. Niven saw the sheriff glance around at all the empty tables as he approached him at the bar.

"Slow day?" Sheriff Long asked as he plopped onto a stool.

"Ain't it always?" Niven joked, making light of his own problems. "What can I get you, Sheriff?"

"The usual," Sheriff Long answered, laying a coin on the bar. He was old for a man with his job and his belly grew rounder with each passing year but if it bothered anyone in Hamner, they kept it to themselves. All one had to do was look into Long's eyes to see that he could still get the job done if need be. He sure didn't lack for courage. About two months ago, three rough, cattle boys had rode into town with a burning need to get drunk and ill intentions. The old man had faced them alone and sent them packing after breaking one's nose and quite likely fracturing another's skull.

Niven liked Sheriff Long. Monday through Saturday, the old man came around at five in the afternoon each day like clockwork. He always ordered at least one drink, sometimes more. Every couple of cents counted with Niven's limited customer base and good customers like Sheriff Long were hard to find. Niven was really grateful for him, especially in this town where offering most folks a shot was like offering them poison.

Sheriff Long downed his glass and plopped it onto the bar. "Tell me, Niven, you seen Harvey lately?"

"Can't say that I have. Think he came in a few weeks ago saying something about heading up into the hills to go boar hunting. Reckon that was the last time I saw him."

"He ain't never come back," Sheriff Long informed him. "His wife's pitching a mighty fit for me to put together a posse and go find him."

Niven leaned onto the bar. "Harvey's a tough fellow. I imagine he's fine and just taking his sweet time up there."

"That's what I said," Sheriff Long grinned. "Couldn't say it to Ruby of course but heck fire, man, if I had a wife like her, I'd need some quiet time too."

They sat in silence for a minute before Niven gave in and asked, "You gonna do it? Go after him, I mean."

"No. At least not yet. If he ain't home by Monday, I'll think on it some more." Sheriff Long rolled a cigarette and lit it up. "Got a telegram this afternoon from over in Boone asking me to get together some men, too. They wanted me to come a-running but didn't say what for. I wrote 'em back to find out more but I didn't never hear nothing more from them yet."

"That's strange." Niven suddenly felt like pouring himself a drink. "What do you think they needed help for?"

"Don't know," Long answered around the cigarette butt rammed between his lips. "Wager it ain't nothing good though. My job's keeping the peace in Hamner. If they can't handle their own problems with malcontents and drunks, that's on them, not me." Sheriff Long fished another coin from his pocket and laid it on the bar. "How about hitting me with another drink there, Niven?"

Niven kept his mouth shut as he reached for the bottle; he could tell Long's mood had turned sour.

* * *

Eileen Johnson sat on the porch staring out into the rows of the front garden. She didn't care what that sad excuse for a sheriff said, Harvey was in trouble somewhere up there in the hills around Hamner. Harvey was a good for nothing, lazy man on occasion but he hadn't done too bad for them. They had their farm to live on and he kept it running. They weren't hurting for anything despite the tab he continued to build up at the saloon in town. His drinking never worried her much as he never hit her and always paid it off in full each season when the crops came in. Eileen wasn't sure that what they shared could be called love but it was better than being alone. If that fool man had gotten himself killed up there, she would be the one who suffered for it, not him. Oh, she would be all right for a year or so with the crop and the money she had saved up without Harvey knowing, but what then? Eileen snorted and continued rocking in her chair. It made her mad but she owed Harvey more than she cared to admit. She couldn't just leave him to rot out there like some animal even if he was dead. Tomorrow, she would hitch up the horses to the wagon and head back into Hamner again. Their farm wasn't that far outside of town and since Harvey had left she'd had to make the trip twice already. That sheriff had another thing coming if he thought she would just cool down and forget about the matter. He got paid to handle things like this, didn't he? She considered taking Harvey's shotgun with her this time. Maybe that would make the sheriff realize just how serious she was. Harvey belonged to her and dead or alive, she wanted him home.

Eileen heard a rumble from somewhere behind the house. It sounded like a windstorm sweeping through the rows of corn back there. She got up and went into the house, listening closely as she made her way to the kitchen. The sun was bright in the sky and there wasn't no wind to speak of. Something was moaning though. She was spooked and she knew it as she fetched the shotgun she had been thinking about. Eileen cracked it open and shoved two shells inside it from the box Harvey kept on his worktable beside the weapon. She slowly tiptoed toward the backdoor of the house.

"Eileen. . ." a cold and raspy voice called to her as the backdoor swung inward. Harvey stood before her, only it wasn't really him. The thing facing her wasn't even human. It looked like her husband but its shirt was smeared with dark, caked blood stains and one of its hands was gone. A jagged edge of white bone protruded from the stump of its right arm where the missing hand would have been. Its head hung sideways at an unnatural angle, resting on its shoulder, though its eyes were alert and burned into her with the hunger she saw in them. The thing took a shambling step into the kitchen, drawing closer to her.

"Harvey Johnson," she warned in a tone that mixed fear and anger, "don't you dare come another step closer or I'll blow you to Hell."

The thing that had been her husband tried to smile, its lips twitching apart on its face. "Eileen," it said again, slurring her name, "I've come home."

She couldn't take it anymore. Eileen shouldered the shotgun, its barrels leveled at the thing's chest, and pulled the trigger. The shotgun thundered, leaving her ears ringing and almost knocking her onto her rear. The blast caught the Harvey-thing dead on, the force of the slugs jerking it up, inches off the floor, and flinging it into the backyard. Eileen threw the empty shotgun at the sink and ran to the doorway. The Harvey-thing lay sprawled in the grass. Its chest was a mess of shattered ribs and mangled meat but it still met her with those hungry eyes. Her breath caught as she saw it trying to get up. The thing that had been her husband should be dead but it was attempting to get to its feet.

"That weren't too nice, Eileen," it wheezed, whistling noises escaping from its ruptured lungs. "Reckon I'll be too slow to be the one who eats you now."

Eileen looked up from the creature to see that it wasn't alone. Several more rotting monsters were stumbling from the fields toward the house. She screamed and retreated into the house, slamming the door. As she turned to try to find the shotgun she'd discarded, she saw them. Five more of the things were in the house with her. They had come in the through the front door while she had been busy with Harvey. The closest one flung itself onto her like it was trying to give her a hug. She tried to shove it away but its cold hands clamped onto her arms. Yellow teeth snapped at her face as she put all her strength into her knee as it rose to meet the dead thing's groin. There was a squishing noise as she made contact and stale blood seeped through the cloth of its pants, but it didn't seem to care. With a snarl, it forced her up against the kitchen wall and sank its teeth into the soft skin of her neck. She watched hot red goo splash onto the wall next to her as pain flowed through her body. Her arms flopped to her sides as she lost her ability to control them. As her world went dark, Eileen could feel the thing gnawing deeper and deeper into her throat as she listened to the smacking sound of the dead man's lips.

* * *

Sheriff Long left Niven's saloon in a fouler mood than he had arrived in. The whiskey only served to put a keener edge on his problems rather than dull them. Something nasty was coming. He could feel it in his bones, but for the life of him he had no idea what it could be. Between Harvey being missing and the strange wire from the next town, he had half a mind to believe it was Indians. There was a tribe or two that lived close enough to be trouble if they really put their minds to it, but in all the years he had been here, they never had.

Sheriff Long was heading up the street to the jail when he saw the rider coming. The figure was pushing his horse like there was no tomorrow. The sun was setting and the shadows stretched across the street as Sheriff Long straightened himself up and walked to meet the man. He flexed his fingers on his gun hand and hoped he wouldn't need the Colt holstered on his hip. The street was empty except for him and the rider. The stores were closed up and most folks he reckoned were in their homes by now.

Long forced himself not to go for his gun as the rider stopped at the last possible instant and leapt out of his saddle. The man's eyes were wild and he stank of fear and desperation. If the man had had a hat, it was gone, likely lost somewhere on the trail into town from his frantic pace. Sweat stained the armpits of blue shirt and dripped from his brow. His skin was horribly sun burnt, rolls of flaking skin covering his cheeks and dried out lips. Sheriff Long didn't recognize the fellow.

The man's gaze was drawn straight to the badge Long had pinned to his chest. "You're the sheriff here?" he asked hurriedly.

Long nodded. Then the man fell forward, likely from sheer exhaustion. Sheriff Long caught him out of instinct. The man was unconscious. Long cursed loudly. The poor horse was in worse shape than its rider. Not only was it pushed to the edge of death from being ridden so hard, but long, deep gashes smeared with blood covered the rear of its right side. It looked as if something had been grabbing for its rider and gotten its hind instead. The horse made it several yards before it keeled over too. Long knew it wouldn't be getting up. The stranger was becoming heavy in his arms and he couldn't leave the dang idiot in the middle of the street. Maybe I am getting too old for this crap after all, Long thought.

It felt like it tore apart every muscle in arms, legs, and back but Long managed to drag the man to the jail. He dropped the man, none too softly, on the jail's floor, hurting badly as he then tried to get him onto one of the beds in the cells. The stranger hadn't stirred in the slightest. He was dead to the world. Long considered leaving him this way until morning but the truth was he needed to know why the man was in such a state and what had brought him to Hamner. Was there trouble on his heels?

There was a bowl of wash water for the prisoners on a nearby table. Long dumped it onto the man. He came to with a start, leaping up as he hand went for his holster.

"Hold up!" Long shouted, his own gun drawn and leveled at the man before he could finish what he had started. "Don't ya do nothing stupid, ya hear?"

The stranger's trembling hand fell to his side. The man clearly wasn't much of a fighter or one of them would be bleeding out on the floor.

"Where am I?" the man asked.

"Don't you know?" Long kept his pistol on the stranger. "You're in Hamner."

"Hamner?" The man repeated the name, then his eyes went wide and the same urgent panic that had filled him before began to creep in again.

"Sheriff, my name is Jeremiah Millsap. I work for the railroad. . .or at least I did. It killed them, Sheriff, like that were nothing. All of them. Just ripped them up. . ."

Long interrupted Jeremiah, "Whoa, son. I think you'd best slow down. I ain't following ya."

* * *

The Family rode west with Sarah in the lead, not Graham. Samuel and Zed rode beside her with the others bringing up the rear.

"Where exactly are we going again?" Zed complained.

"I don't know," Sarah answered him, annoyed by his constant badgering. "I just know we need to go this way."

"I got to admit, it ain't like Graham to let someone else take the lead." Zed nodded back in the direction of where Graham rode behind them.

"Graham knew that whatever lies ahead must be dealt with if it was powerful enough that Samuel and I both felt it," Sarah explained.

"Okay, Samuel, I got that you're all in tune with the mystical world and such," Zed lit up a smoke, "but why would Sarah sense whatever is out there?"

"Sarah is connected to the energies the humans falsely think of as the Greek gods. Her talents come from the forces the humans refer to as Athena and Ares. Something powerful that should not be, has awakened. I believe that Sarah has been summoned to stop this evil before it spreads farther than it already has. Even now, I can feel it growing," Samuel licked his lips. "If it could be trapped, channeled in a proper fashion. . ."

"No," Sarah growled. "Whatever is out there, Samuel, it has to be destroyed, wiped completely off the face of the Earth. Like you said, it should not be."

Zed took a drag from his cigarette and blow smoke into the wind. "I'll never understand all this supernatural voodoo. Just give me my guns and a target. That's all I need to get the job done."

Samuel laughed. Sarah gave him a sharp look. "It's all right, Zed. I don't understand it either but we have to do this. You trust me on that don't you?"

"You know I do, sis," Zed nodded, "but I still don't have to like it."

Suddenly the wind changed direction. The smell of death and rot washed over them so strong that even Samuel gagged.

"What the devil is that?" Graham called from behind them.

"The enemy," Sarah and Zed heard Samuel say quietly in a voice barely above a whisper.

Ahead of them, three men and two women came up the road. All of them were on foot and their movements were twitchy and unnatural, almost as if they were puppets dancing on the strings of unseen fingers. The men and women blocked the road.

"Are they dead?" Zed asked. "They sure look dead to me."

The flesh of the men and women was ripe with decay. White, fat maggots swam over and across a long gash on the center man's cheek. All of the dead were marked by at least one noticeable wound and their eyes were cold and hollow, devoid of emotion or anything that would constitute a soul.

The man in the center raised a hand with three fingers and the mangled stump of a fourth one at them. His thumb was missing and the skin around where it should have been looked like it had been chewed upon.

"Turn back," the man said in a voice that sounded like the hull of a boat crunching on gravel. "You are not welcome here."

The rest of the Family rode up, forming a line with Sarah and Samuel in its center.

"What are those things?" Graham asked just as calm and collected as he always was.

"Revenants," Samuel snarled.

"You mean they're undead?" Shannon asked, though he appeared to already know the answer.

"Don't much care what they are," Yule roared. "Ain't nobody tells us what to do."

Before anyone could stop him, Yule was off his horse and wading into the group of dead men and woman blocking their path.

"Wait, Yule!" Sarah yelled, but the giant wasn't listening.

Yule plowed into the dead like a juggernaut. His swift punch went clean through the first man's chest, his fist exploding from the man's back in a shower of goo and black blood. Yule yanked his arm free, nearly ripping the dead man in half in the process. The wound would have been instantly fatal to a living person but the dead man stayed on his feet, swaying back and forth, trying to keep himself upright despite his shattered spine. Yule's second punch splattered open one of the women's guts sending her sprawling onto her butt. Neither of the two dead Yule had struck appeared to feel even the slightest hint of pain. The other three dead humans sprang at Yule as one, their teeth snapping. A barrage of bullets from Zed's Colts sent them stumbling backward, leaking black blood.

"Dang it!" Zed shouted. "Those bastards are hard to kill!"

"They are already dead," Samuel reminded the others. "You must take their heads or destroy their brains to return them to the Hell that gave them birth."

Sarah saw Zed stare at Samuel, his mouth hanging open. "Well you could have told me that a bit sooner. Bullets cost money, ya know?"

"You will not be warned again," the man with the broken spine rasped as his precarious balance finally gave way and his top half slid apart from his legs, attached only by the thinnest strands of muscles and skin to flop into the dirt of the road. The others were moving toward Yule again as the giant retreated from them and their grasping hands. Zed popped off five hurried shots, burying a bullet in each of the dead men and women's skulls. This time, none of them got up or moved again.

Graham shook his head in disgust, wiping at a spot of brain matter on his sleeve that had splashed there from the closer creatures. "You sure know how to pick an interesting mess to get us into, Sarah," he turned to glance at Samuel. "There's gonna be a lot more of these things aren't there?"

"That you can count on," Samuel answered grimly.

* * *

Heather stood at the edge of the loft, looking down into the fields below the barn. Nothing in the world made sense anymore. She and the Hyatt brothers had been down at the creek fishing and passing the afternoon when the older brother, Weldon, had caught something big on his line. At first, none of them knew what it was. The water wasn't very clear and they'd been excited, hoping and judging by the struggle that it was going to be the biggest catch on record in the town. It had taken all the strength Weldon and Jerry could manage to pull the thing in, only it hadn't been a fish at all. A man, dead and bloated, emerged from the murky water as they yanked it onto the bank. The brothers had dropped their pole and scrambled away from the body as it did the impossible and opened its eyes. In a water-logged voice that splashed mud and grime from its lungs, the thing laughed, "Good boys. I'm so very hungry. I've been down there on the bottom for a quite a spell."

The dead man sprang up, with surprising speed, to grab a hold on Weldon's leg. The dead man's jagged fingernails tore at the cloth of Weldon's pants and through it to the soft skin of his inner thigh as it pulled itself forward. Weldon howled like a cat with its tail caught in the kitchen door as the dead man's teeth sank into his leg just below his knee. Heather kept herself from screaming as Jerry snatched up a huge rock and cracked the dead man over the head. She heard bone cave inward from the blow and the dead man slumped into the mud of the creek's bank. Weldon clawed his way free from the corpse's hold as blood poured from the bite on his leg, staining his torn pants.

"Oh Lord, oh Lord," Weldon was begging as she and Jerry helped him to his feet. They had heard movement in the woods around them. More things like the man they had pulled from the water were coming out into the open. The creatures were shambling quickly through the trees towards the spot where the three of them stood.

"We have to run," she told the Hyatt brothers. Sweat was forming on Weldon's face and brow as he grew paler with each passing second.

"I can't!" Weldon cried before he was seized by a coughing fit that ended with blood coming out of his nose as his body shook violently.

Jerry met her eyes. "I won't leave him," he told her firmly. "He's my brother."

"I'm sorry," Heather told them and meant it. . . Then she had to run. Not just run but run for her life. Heather left the Hyatt brothers standing there as the dead closed in on them. Heather never looked back, she was too afraid of what she would see but she heard the brothers screaming as she darted through the woods, ducking low limbs and jumping over thick roots that poked up through the forest floor around the thickest trees.

An hour later, she reached the Hall farm. It wasn't much farther to town but she couldn't go on. Each labored, exhausted breath she took burnt her throat and lungs. Her legs felt as if they would give way at any moment. As she neared the farm, she thought about yelling for help but something insider her kept her silent. The door to the Hall's house flopped open, swinging on its hinges in the late afternoon breeze. The clouds above were dark and a storm was closing in from the distant mountains. Heather slowed her pace, nearly collapsing in the process. There was blood pooled beneath the swinging door and more smeared onto the wall of the house beside it. Her tears broke loose like a dam giving way. They slid over her cheeks and blurred her vision. Though by then, she had spotted the Hall's barn and made for it. Inside its thick walls, horses lay gutted and partially eaten in their stables. The smell of their bowels lying in the hay pushed her to the edge of vomiting. She didn't stop to examine the poor animals any more closely than that first passing glance. She knew if she did, she would have lose it.

Fighting against waves of nausea from the smell alone and her exhaustion, she scampered up into the barn's loft and held herself, letting time pass.

She been hiding here ever since. She didn't know how much time had gone by, hours maybe? She had gotten her strength back some and moved to the edge of the loft where she stood now. Heather couldn't see any of the dead in the farm's large yard or in the fields but she could hear their inhuman cries and snarls in the distance. Were the things still hunting for her? She didn't know, but she did know that if she stayed here and they found her, she was dead. The things would trap her up here in the loft until they could overrun her and rip her apart with their teeth and nails like they had the animals. Her only hope was to get back to town and find her father. He would know what to do and if he didn't, she knew where he kept his shotgun hidden under the saloon's bar.

* * *

Night had fallen over Hamner. A light rain was falling. Niven stood behind the bar staring out the saloon's door into the street beyond. Not a single soul had come along since Sheriff Long had left. Sure, he never had had many customers but this evening things were quite . . .dead. He couldn't even remember the last person, other than the Sheriff, he had seen go by. Where was everybody? Even for Hamner, it was downright strange. Maybe the threat of bad weather was keeping everyone in. He shrugged to himself and left the bar, walking over to the saloon's main door. Heather should be in soon, he reckoned. He had told her to be home before dark, which usually meant she would show up half an hour or so after the sun sank from the sky with one excuse or another as to why she was late. If he questioned her on it, she would just remind him he still hadn't bought her that horse he had promised her on her birthday.

With a half-smile at the thought of his daughter's tomboy arrogance, Niven stepped into the street to get a better look up and down its expanse. The only light he saw came from the jail. The flicking glow of a lamp lit its sole window. The rain began to pick up, not into a full out downpour, but it growing steady and harder. He could just barely hear something over it. Something that reminded him of a man moaning. He found himself wondering what kind of idiot would be out in this weather, then felt the rain pounding against his hair and shoulders and realized that he was that kind of idiot.

Niven turned and headed back into the saloon, letting the doors swing shut behind him. He shook off the rain as best he could and hoped Heather had one heck of an excuse tonight because she was going to need it. She might be a young woman now but he would take her over his knee and blister her bottom if she got sick from being out in this weather.

A clinking of glasses from behind the saloon's bar stirred Niven from his thoughts. As his head rose, Niven saw them. Seven men and half-a-dozen women filled the wide space of the saloon's main room. Each and every one of them was soaked from the rain. Their hungry eyes fell upon him as he saw that they were messed up. Heck, they were dead, dead and walking. Some of them were almost normal enough to pass as alive but their hollow stares and blood-smeared mouths betrayed them. The others were visibly rotting and covered in wounds. Niven backed up a step towards the door but they swung apart as more of the creatures entered the saloon, trapping him between them and the others. A chorus of moans arose among them. Niven was a big man, though more fat than muscle, but he was far from helpless. He grabbed up a chair from a nearby table as the creatures came at him.

"Get back!" he yelled.

A man with bullet holes riddling his red, stained shirt was the first to reach him. Niven swung the chair, breaking it over the thing that had once been a man. The dead man slumped to the floor, small pieces of the chair's splintered wood drawn into its gray flesh. The thing looked up at him as it moaning grew louder. Niven drove a balled-up fist down onto the top of its skull, grunting from the force of his effort. The creature thumped back onto the floor, then Niven was moving. He charged forward through the dead, punching and shoving them from his path as he raced for the bar and the shotgun that waited there. One of the dead women flung herself onto his back. She shrieked like a banshee as her nails raked at his cheek and clawed over his scalp. His own blood ran down into his eyes and mouth. He tasted its salty, coppery flavor and spat red. Reaching over his shoulder, Niven grabbed the dead woman by her hair and slung her over him to the floor. She landed flat on her back with the crunching sound of bones breaking against the hard wood below her.

Niven jumped over her twitching form and kept going. Two of the men met him head on just short of the bar. They barreled into him, knocking him off balance. All three of them went down in an entangled mass of struggling limbs. Niven screamed as one of the men bit off his right ear. The other man went for his nose but Niven flung his own head forward, smashing the man's teeth inward with his forehead. Niven managed to throw one of the men away from him but the effort was useless. Three more of the creatures dropped onto him in the man's place. Jagged nails dug into the skin of his neck and one of the men sank yellow teeth into Niven's ankle. Still Niven fought on. He knew if he died, these things would be waiting for Heather when she came home. He couldn't bring himself to even consider the fact that they could have gotten her already.

He changed his tactics, no longer concerned with whether he lived or died, instead focusing on killing as many of the blasted things as he could. His hands latched onto the sides of a dead woman's head and he snapped her neck with a quick twist. She did not move again. Niven laughed through his pain, frantically finding a new wave of strength. As the creatures ripped and tore at him, he rolled over, pinning one of the men beneath him, pushing his thumbs into its eyes until there was a popping noise and his fingers were deep inside the thing's skull.

The teeth of one of the dead women found Niven's groin. He squealed like a rabid pig as she chewed on his manhood. His body became a mangled mess from the creatures' continued and relentless assault and in seconds the blackness took him. Niven's final thoughts were of Heather as he passed from this world.

* * *

Sheriff Long stared across his desk at Jeremiah. "Say again? I didn't quite get that, son."

"You heard me, sheriff. The dead are hungry you see? Everyone that monster kills gets up and starts killing themselves and the folks they kill do the same. Think of it like a disease. The monster is spreading its evil. It wants the whole world to be like it, worship it. I didn't mean to set it loose. Hell, I don't even know what is but I can tell you it's coming, sheriff, its children with it. . . If it isn't here already."

"That's one whopper of a story, boy. I don't know if I should lock you up or put a bullet in you for your own good." Sheriff Long leaned against the wall behind his desk in his chair. Jeremiah's expression grew more intense with desperation and fear.

"We have got to stop it, sheriff. Those folks asleep out there in your town that you're sworn to watch over will be dead, worse than dead, if we don't."

"Look, boy, what exactly do you want me to do? There ain't been no trouble here that I know of. Am I supposed to break out the rifles over there" Long pointed at a gun case on the jail's wall, "and go house to house handing them out while I tell folks Hell its self is coming for them?"

"That would be a good start," Jeremiah said.

Long got up and walked to the window, peering out into the street. "Don't suppose you got any proof of your claims?" Long asked. "What you're asking me to do is plumb crazy, boy. You know that, don't you?"

"Yes, sir," Jeremiah answered, "but it still needs to be done."

"There's riders coming in," Long said. "Six of them if I count right through the rain. They with you?"

Jeremiah was on his feet. "No. I suggest you get away from there before they see you. If they're dead, we're gonna have fight on our hands."

Long grunted. "I never said I believed you, boy, but this is my town. You wait here. I'm gonna go see who they are."

"Don't," Jeremiah warned, but Long went out the door into the street without so much as glancing back.

* * *

Rain fell hard as the Family rode into Hamner. Samuel smelled the rot of the creatures even through the rain. There was power here in this town, such power. He felt it in his bones. Since the Family had encountered a group of the undead hours before on the road here he had been raking his brain trying to figure out exactly what they might be up against. All his life, he had walked the spirit worlds and sought knowledge and magic lost to this modern world of science. Now with the power so thick about him, he knew. Atune was the entity's name. It was a demon that most had forgotten. A demon whose sole purpose was to tear asunder the world of man and burn it to the ground. It was not subtle like its master Lucifer nor did it enjoy games with the mortals, toying with their emotions like its brothers in the form of Legion. No, it was more like the ancient Malamon, but without Malamon's true apocalyptic reach. To spread its taint, it needed the creatures it created, needed then ones those creatures killed. Stopping Atune would be challenging, but the demon was well within the Family's ability to deal with.

Samuel wondered briefly if Atune *should* be stopped. The demon held no quarrel against the Family or their kind, only the humans created in God's image. Perhaps they should let Atune finish his work upon the world before they slew him. Samuel sighed loudly. There would be no chance of that. Even Sarah, as lethal and cold as she was towards humanity, still wouldn't slay a human without cause, however slight that cause may be. Shannon and Zed would willingly and wholeheartedly leap to the human's defense. Yule would follow Zed's lead as he always did and Graham, Graham hated change. He thrived on order and fixed things that he believed he could control. There would be no controlling Atune, and the Earth would be a different world if the demon was allowed to complete its goal.

"It's here," Sarah told them all. "I can feel it all around us."

Zed was on edge, clearly ready for a fight.

"How do we find it?" Graham asked.

"I wouldn't worry about that, brother," Samuel laughed. "It will find us when it's ready."

The street of the town was deserted as they rode along it in the rain. Ahead of them, the door of the jail opened and a man in his late fifties wearing a gleaming silver badge came out to meet them.

"Y'all hold it right there now," the sheriff ordered them, a Winchester leveled in their direction.

Samuel snorted as Graham and Sarah moved their horses slightly forward to speak with the sheriff.

"Hello," Graham said, paying no heed to the man's rifle. "I'm Graham Farr and these are my brothers and sister."

"Don't care who you are," the sheriff spat. "You ain't dead at least."

"Dead?" Graham teased.

"Don't play smart with me, boy. You're with that idiot I got in the jail aren't you? I don't know what y'all are trying to pull here but us folks in Hamner don't want no part of it. You just turn those horses around and ride out like you came in and maybe I'll let your friend go to join you in a bit."

"You're a fool," Samuel growled at the sheriff.

Graham gave Samuel a disapproving glance as the sheriff raised his Winchester to his shoulder and took proper aim at the wizard wolf in black robes. Samuel's eyes were full of nothing but contempt.

"We're only here to help," Sarah said quietly, trying to defuse the situation. "We don't want any trouble that doesn't have to be."

"You're a mighty fine looking woman," the sheriff told her, "but there's six of you and one of me so you'll forgive me if I don't take your claim on faith."

"Put the rifle down and let's be reasonable," Graham purred.

Samuel felt his hackles rise. Graham was using his talent for controlling others. It stunk in Samuel's nostrils like rancid meat as he shook off the waves of calm Graham was emitting. The human sheriff however lacked the willpower to do so. He lowered his rifle slowly, staring at Graham.

"Dang me, son, if I don't believe you," the sheriff said. "I'm getting too old for all the killing this job brings with it anyway. If you wanna talk, my ears are open. Just tell me why the Hell y'all are here?"

A girl, with hair as red as Sarah's, came running up the street from the other side of the town towards them.

"Run!" she screamed. "They're coming!"

The girl wore pants like a boy and her cheeks were covered in freckles. Her clothes were a mess, torn and picked at, and she looked so exhausted it was a minor miracle she was still standing. Sarah could see fear was pushing her on.

Behind the girl, a small army of shambling dead men, women, and children give chase.

"We're surrounded," Zed announced so sharply and out of the blue that Sarah flinched in her saddle.

Samuel looked at Graham and said, "The demon comes."

"And it looks like the whole town is a coming with him," Yule roared, drawing the heavy shotgun sheathed on his horse's saddle.

"Can those things hurt us?" Graham demanded, yelling at Samuel and Sarah.

Sarah shrugged. She was a warrior not a mage.

"Yes," Samuel said, "though not easily. I don't believe their infection will spread to us unless they're able to inflict what would be a mortal wound to a human."

"Still," Zed said, "there's too many of them things to make a stand in the open like this."

The sheriff seemed to have forgotten about the Family entirely, sweeping his head from side to side in shock, taking in the sea of hungry, gray faces closing in on them all. He snapped out of his horror as Graham shouted, "Into the jail! Sarah, Zed, get that girl before those things do!"

The Family dismounted, scattering their horses and sending the beasts running, as they all sprinted for the jail's door except for Sarah and Zed.

Seeing the girl running towards her was like looking into a warped mirror as Sarah raced to meet her. Yule and Shannon started laying down cover fire as they waited just outside the jail on opposite sides of its doorway. Yule's shotgun thundered, blowing a gaping hole in a dead man's chest before Shannon reminded him, "The head, Yule! You have to shoot them in the head!"

Shannon popped off two shots, dropping a one-eyed woman with half a face and a man dressed in the simple clothes of a farmer who had no lower jaw. Zed sped past Sarah, swooping up the girl in his arm. Sarah drew her sword as a man with only one arm came lumbering at her, his teeth snapping at empty air in anticipation of the taste of her flesh and the flavor of her blood on his tongue. Sarah growled, her eyes glowing yellow with rage, as she lashed out with supernatural strength and her blade cut the dead man in half at the waist. She crunched in his skull with the heel of one of her heavy boots as she stepped over him to meet three more of the dead. Her sword flashed in the rain, taking heads and slicing into brain matter. In seconds, nine motionless bodies lay around her in the street. But that number was next to nothing compared to the amount of bloodied corpses that still stumbled forward.

"Sarah!" she heard Shannon yell for her. The bloodlust pulsing through her veins dimmed enough for her to realize that the others were inside the jail now expect for herself and Shannon, who held the door for her. She spun and made for the jail. The horde of dead creatures moaned and snarled as they followed after her. As soon as Sarah was through the doorway, Shannon slammed the door in the faces of the dead.

"Anyone got a plan?" Zed asked, holding the redheaded girl in his arms as several pairs of rotting hands burst through the jail's window, shards of broken glass clattering onto the floor below it. Yule moved to the window, shoving his large shotgun into the dead faces and squeezing the trigger. The booming it made while it emptied its barrels seemed to shake the jail.

"Yeah," Yule grunted in a low voice, "keep those thing the Hell out!"

Zed darted into one of the open cells and gently laid the girl on its bed. The girl was unconscious now, whether from fear or exhaustion was anyone's guess. The sheriff yanked a bottle of whiskey from a drawer in his desk and kicked it back, draining a good portion of what remained in it. "Dang!" the sheriff bellowed, shaking his head. "It's all real, ain't it? The dead are walking! It's the end of the world."

"Do shut up," Samuel said and gave him a vicious backhanded slap. The force of it fractured the sheriff's skull and he slumped to the floor leaking blood from his nose and ears that pooled around him where he fell.

"Samuel!" Shannon challenged his black-robed brother.

"Forgive me," Samuel held up his hands in a gesture of peace. "But he had it coming."

Graham got everyone's attention as he yelled, "That door ain't gonna hold 'em! Yule, help me get something in front of it!"

Yule sealed up the breech of his reloaded shotgun and kicked the sheriff's desk over to block the door to the street.

As suddenly as it began, the attack on the jail came to a halt.

"What the . . .?" Zed muttered.

"Atune," Samuel whispered.

* * *

In the street outside, the dead backed away from the walls of the jail as their ranks parted and a ten-foot-tall demon with bleeding skin came forward.

"Little wolves," it shouted, "must we be enemies? Surrender the humans to me and you may go on your way unharmed."

The young man who had been waiting in the jail when the Family had rushed inside sat in a corner whimpering with tears streaming down his cheeks. Graham grabbed him by the front of his shirt, lifting him from the floor. "Give me one good reason we shouldn't just leave you to die?"

"It would be wrong," Shannon answered for the young man. "And that thing out there won't stop with this town. You know that, Graham."

"There is however something to be said for an orderly withdrawal from the field," Samuel argued.

"I ain't running," Yule put his foot down. "Let's go kill that thing and get it over with!"

"Wolves!" the demon called again. "My patience is at an end. What is your answer?"

Sarah decided for the others. She shoved the heavy desk aside and kicked the jail's door so hard shards of its shattering wood rained out onto the muddy street.

"Today, demon," she snarled from the jail's doorway, "today is the day you die."

The demon laughed then nodded. "So be it, little wolves. Come out and face me if you dare."

Sarah gave a howling battle cry and rushed towards the demon as the others followed her out of the jail. The dead held back, waiting on their master to give them the word to take action, as Sarah leaped through the air, swinging her sword at the demon's face. It caught her blade mid-swing in scythe-like talons and wrenched it from her grasp. Its other hand snaked out to close fingers around her throat. The demon held her two feet above the ground to its side as the rest of the Family came at it. Zed emptied his twin Colts into the demon's chest, his final shot going higher to slam into its forehead. Though more blood poured from its already-bleeding skin than from the wounds, the bullets had no real effect on the demon. Sarah clawed at its wrist, trying desperately to break its hold on her as hair grew over her exposed skin and her clothes tore and ripped, her muscles growing underneath them. Her lower jaw extended as she snarled, extending razor sharp teeth. The demon flung her aside as Yule rushed it. Laughing, it met the big man head on. Yule and the demon crashed into one another like runaway locomotives. Their arms locked like wrestlers, each trying to push the other back. At first, they seemed caught in a standstill of equally matched strength, but then the demon twisted, flinging Yule about to lift the big man over its head. The demon tossed Yule into Graham, sending them both rolling through the mud.

Shannon sprang at the demon in his hybrid form, all white fur, muscle, and snarling teeth. His claws raked the demon across its face. The demon staggered a step but quickly recovered, eyes burning bright red, filled with hate and anger. It snatched Shannon by his right arm, breaking it in the process, and pulled him close. Shannon's teeth snapped at the demon but the entity held the white wolf where Shannon's jaws were just out of reach. One of the demon's massive fists smashed into

Shannon's jaw, sending teeth flying. It dropped Shannon's unconscious form at its feet and looked up to find Samuel grinning at it.

"Atune," Samuel called it by its true name.

"You know me?" the demon rasped.

Samuel took a step forward, his hands weaving strange patterns in the air before him. "I know you, demon," Samuel chuckled, "and I am your better. Run now and I might let you live."

With a furious roar, the demon hurled itself at the black-robed wolfman. An orb of crackling blue energy formed between Samuel's hands. It flew into the demon, searing its flesh, and knocking it onto its butt in the mud.

"Impressive, little wolf," the demon purred. "You are stronger than I would have imagined, but still not strong enough."

Like a tentacle, the demon's tongue shot from its distending jaws to curl about Samuel's throat, cutting off his breath. Samuel clawed at the tongue with both hands as his cheeks grew blue and he suffocated from the pressure constricting him..

"No!" Sarah cried. She was human once more, naked, and armed with her sword. Her blade came out of nowhere and slashed the demon's tongue in two. The half still entangling Samuel fell limp while the other half recoiled into the demon's mouth like a snapping whip. The demon whined in pain.

"Bitch!" it wailed at her. "You hurt me! For that, you will die slowly as I enjoy every hole your soft flesh has to offer."

"I don't think so," Zed told it. Though Shannon remained unconscious, sprawled out in the middle of the street, her other brothers stood with Zed. "Sam here says you can die. I think we are just the fellows to make that happen."

Distracted by the male members of the Family, the demon never saw Sarah coming at it again until it was too late. Its head left its body in a spray of blood and pus as Sarah's blade sliced through the flesh and bone of its neck.

"Destroy the body!" Samuel yelled at Zed.

The speedster moved like lightning flashing the sky, transforming into his hybrid form as he went. He grabbed the demon's body and dragged it along the street towards the church at the edge of town. With a strained grunt, Zed heaved the demon's body at the church. It burst into flames as it flew over the holy ground and only ashes remained to strike the church's wall before they scattered into the night.

Sarah walked over to where the demon's head lay. It was mouthing a stream of silent curses at her as it had no lungs to give its words life. Sarah sank her blade downward through the top of its skull. What remained of its tongue flopped from its mouth as its eyes rolled up to show only whites.

As one, the surrounding horde of dead folks gave a final moan and collapsed to lay unmoving around them as the Family watched.

"It's dead," Samuel announced, rubbing at the flayed skin of his neck.

"Thank God," Sarah sighed and sank to her knees. "It's over."

POSTSCRIPT

HEATHER AWOKE IN AN UNLOCKED JAIL CELL. SHE came awake with a start. Her clothes were filthy and stained with blood. The last thing she remembered were monsters chasing her through the street. Sunlight was pouring through the shattered window on the far wall outside the cell. She leapt to her feet. The door of the jail lay in pieces and she could see the blue sky through it even from where she stood. The sheriff's corpse was surrounded by a pool congealed red, his final resting place, a spot on the jail's floor near where his desk usually sat. It was all real. The Hyatt brothers, the Halls, and who knew how many more were dead. Her eyes scanned the room for a weapon. There was an open case of rifles on the wall. She took one down and to her surprise, it was loaded. Whatever else you said about Sheriff Long, he'd always liked to be prepared.

Taking a moment to gather her courage, Heather walked out of the jail into the wet street. The smell was horrible. Despite the dripping of last nights' rain off the eaves of the surrounding buildings, it was a beautiful day…except for the hundreds of corpses that filled the street of Hamner. A small gasp escaped her lips as she stood in awe of the carnage. So many bodies, she thought. Dogs roamed among the dead, sniffing and sometimes stopping eat from them. Heather walked among the bodies searching. She could not find her father. What she did find, upon entering the saloon, was body parts, and bloodied scraps of her father's bar apron.

Over the next hour she called for others but got no reply. The open sky and rays of sun somehow told her she was alone now. There was no one else.

The man who had saved her the night before was not among the dead and she saw no trace of the others he'd been with. . That gave her hope that there were folks other than herself who were still alive in the world. He must have survived, unlike her father.

Tears burned her eyes but she quickly wiped them away, refusing to lose focus right now. There had been enough crying already. For the moment, she was safe. She hoped all of the rotting creatures had met their end like these ones around her but who knew anything in this crazy world anymore?

Heather headed for the stables, hoping to find a horse that had survived the night. Her life here was gone. With a horse and all the money she could ever need sitting alone in Hamner's bank, making a new start would be easy enough. However, she swore she was going to find that man from the night before first. She owed him her life and he owed her an explanation of what had happened here and why her father had been killed. No matter what it took or how long she had to search, she *would* find him. She knew what he looked like and if she recalled correctly, his name was Zed.

PART TWO

A Pack Of Wolves

"**G**ET IN THE HOUSE!" SHARON SCREAMED, SHOVING Graham, the closest of the children, on towards the door. The men were coming, riding hard and fast across the open plain. David loaded his musket then grabbed two pistols, shoving them under his belt as he came out onto the porch. He stood watching his wife trying to herd the children inside past him.

Yule stared up at him. He was the biggest of the lot. "Let me fight, Dad. I can help you."

David ruffled his hair. "No, son. You get on inside with the others."

"But, Dad!" Yule argued.

"Now, Yule!" David ordered. Little Zed, the smallest and so thin he looked like he was being starved to death despite eating like a horse, took Yule by the arm and tugged on him.

"Yule, leave Dad alone. He can handle this," Zed wailed.

Sharon came up the steps of the porch with Shannon and Sarah, dragging each of them by a hand. She stopped in front of David. "Do we need to run?"

David counted the number of riders again. There were fourteen of them. He shook his head. "I knew the church was after us but I didn't really expect them to come," he said sadly. "Not after all this time. I'm sorry."

Sharon gave him a peck on the cheek. "The Lord will watch us," she told him. He stared at her wondering how she could still have faith when the Lord's supposed servants on Earth wanted their blood so badly.

"I love you," he said and stepped off the porch to meet the riders.

"Daddy!" Sarah yelled, trying to break free of her mother's hold.

Though it hurt him to do so, David ignored her cries. The riders were close now. They came galloping up and stopped in front of him. They were all dressed in black except one man who wore white from head to toe. One of the men in black moved forward, bringing his horse just a tad closer. He had a grey beard and a silver cross dangling from a chain around his neck,

"Are you David Farr?" the man asked.

"And what if I am?" David answered. "I ain't done nothing wrong and this here is my property you're on."

The man laughed. "All of this world belongs to the Lord and we are his servants. We've traveled a long way to find you, Mr. Farr."

David saw that Sharon had gotten the kids and herself inside. "My family's in the house. I have children. Can't you just leave us alone? Like I said, we ain't hurting nobody."

The priest shook his head. "You stink of animal lust and the blood of your last kill. Your kind cannot be allowed to live."

David realized there would be no reasoning with these men. Snarling, he jerked up his musket and blew a hole in the priest's chest, sending him toppling from his horse.

The other men panicked. Some of their horses were spooked by the shot. The man dressed in white behind them was totally calm. He met David's eyes and smiled like they were neighbors sharing a pew on Sunday morning. The coldness in those eyes sent a shiver down David's spine. He yanked his two pistols from his belt and put a shot into the closest of the men in black. The young man he hit in the side, screamed, and thudded to the ground from his rearing horse. David whipped his last pistol around at one of the men who had a scar running over his left eye but before he could fire a silver mini-ball ripped through his shoulder. David roared against the pain, his teeth becoming razors inside his mouth. He let the change happen instead of trying to fight it. These men knew what he and his family were. That was why they were here. Dark hair sprouted on his skin as his head shook and pain like fire coursed through his veins. He grew two feet taller as his bones reshaped themselves and his muscles grew denser.

David was ready to rend their flesh with his claws until none of the men were recognizable even by their own families but he never got the chance. Several of the men's muskets cracked in unison. David staggered as their shots tore into him. He reeled about to face the house and howled, "Run!"

He reverted to human form and lay in the grass bleeding, unable to move and help his family. The priests in black rushed by him on foot, bloodlust in their eyes. "No," he begged weakly. He found his faith again as he tried to crawl towards the house on his stomach, blood pouring from his multiple wounds. He said a prayer, asking the Lord to spare his children.

The man in white stood above him. David stared up at him. "Why?" he croaked.

"They think you're demons," the man in white snickered. "Maybe we'll see each other again in Hell someday." He blew David a kiss then leveled a pistol at David's face and pulled the trigger.

That muzzle flash was the last thing David Farr ever saw.

* * *

Zed stared across the table at the fat man in the little brown hat. All the other players were out of the game, folded because of the stakes.

There was over five hundred dollars in the pot and Zed's own revolvers. He'd offered them up to stay in the game. Zed glanced at the bar. Yule sat on one of the stools. Only God knew how much whiskey his big brother had downed tonight. A large breasted brunette sat next to Yule as he cradled a slim blonde in his lap. Yule might be as dumb as a pile of bricks but his size and hard muscles always drew the ladies to him like flies to meat no matter where they traveled. Zed shook his head, turning his attention back to his cards. All he held was a pair of aces.

Noticing his expression, the fat man rasped in a phlegm-filled voice, "You in or out?"

Zed sniffed the air. The scent of the fat man's confidence was so powerful he could smell it over the cloud of smoke in the bar. He knew he was beat. He could fold, cut his losses, and walk away but where would the fun be in that? Yule would never forgive him.

"I'm in and I call," Zed smiled, spreading his cards onto the table in front of him.

Laughing, the fat man laid down a royal flush. "Too bad for you." The fat man leaned forward, sweeping the huge pot towards him. He lifted one of Zed's revolvers, inspecting its custom-made grip.

"Hold up," Zed said. "I don't care about the money but you ain't taking my guns."

The fat man nodded at two ranch hands at the next table. They stood and walked over to stand near him. "You lost them fair and square, son. A man has to honor his debts."

Zed knew the fat man was a big wig in this town. Supposedly, he owned most of it too. A man like that never left his ranch alone. Zed imagined the two idiots standing next to him weren't the only protection he had in the bar. The ranch hands eased their fists towards the holsters on their belts.

"Just give me the guns," Zed warned them.

"Look," the fat man told him, "I'm sure none of us here wants any trouble. Ain't that right, Hank?"

The larger of the two ranch hands grunted, spitting a mouthful of tobacco juice onto the floor. "No, sir, that'd be downright foolish, wouldn't it, pup?"

Anger flashed through Zed. "What did you call me, mister?"

Zed's eyes blazed yellow, glowing in the shadows of the bar's low light. The fat man was on his feet, backing away from the table, holding Zed's guns and staring at him with holy terror in his eyes. His two lackeys drew their guns, leveling them at Zed. This was going to get bloody.

"What in the hell are you?" the fat man squealed.

Zed leapt over the table as the two ranch hands opened fire. The bullets came at him in slow motion. Zed caught them both easily as he flipped through the air to land in front of the men. He grinned, showing them their bullets lying in his open palms.

The whole bar erupted into chaos at the shots. The showgirls were running for the stairs, the bartender was reaching for a concealed weapon of some sort, and most of the men were getting to their feet, guns drawn. The rest of the crowd was busy taking cover under their tables or making a bee line for the door.

"It's about time," Yule roared. "I thought we'd never get to the fighting part." His thunderous voice echoed off the bar's walls, shaking the glass in the windows. The poor bartender was so frightened that he emptied both barrels of the shotgun in his trembling hands into Yule's back out of sheer panic. That shot set loose a chorus of others as everyone in the bar fought to make it out alive. No one except Zed and the fat man's party really knew what was happening but no one wanted to die. Bullets flew everywhere and men screamed as the bar became a war zone.

The blast from the shotgun knocked Yule from his stool. Zed saw his big brother's bleeding and mangled back healing as he went after the bartender with bared, razor-like teeth and a loud, angry growl. Zed moved like lightning in the sky, dodging one bullet after another until he was in the fat man's face. He calmly took his revolvers from the fat man's hands and shot him point blank in his rolling gut. Before the fat man's body even hit the floor, Zed was moving again. His guns blazed. Both of the ranch hands' foreheads caved inward as Zed put three rounds into each of them. Zed ran between their falling bodies, passing them, and up onto the wall of the bar. The wood splintered in his wake, spraying tiny fragments of splintered shrapnel as the other men in the bar tried to take him down, their bullets smacking into it.

Zed's feet touched the ceiling as he spun, twisting about, his guns blazing. Another four men were dead as he landed in a crouch on the floor with his revolvers empty and their barrels smoking. The upper half of the bartender lay a few feet from him, strands of entrails leaking from the lower part of his torso where his legs should have been. Yule was finishing up the last of the bar's patrons who were too stupid to run. He stood seven feet tall, towering over a cowboy in a long duster who had two six-guns leveled at him. The pistols spat lead. Yule grunted as each bullet ripped into his massive, hairy chest. The cowboy managed to get off five shots before Yule's hand closed around his head and popped it like an overripe melon underneath his hat. Blood and brain matter sprayed from the cowboy's eyes, ears, and nose. Yule let the cowboy's corpse flop with a dull thud to land at his feet. Yule's eyes were red orbs of pure violence as he searched for someone else to kill.

"I think that's enough, boys," a man in a fine black suit called to them. He was smoking a cigar as he leaned against the frame of the bar's doorway,

Zed couldn't believe his eyes. "Graham?" he said.

Yule charged at Graham but a slim, beautiful redhead in the clothes of gunfighter slipped through the door to stand between the two of them. Yule yelped, skidding to a halt. His eyes going wide with fear. Zed burst into laughter. "Sarah!" he yelled. In a blink, he had her in his arms, spinning her around in a wild embrace. Graham puffed on his cigar as he put Sarah down.

"Been a long time," Sarah said, "I see you boys still love your trouble."

"We didn't start it," Zed tried to explain. "That fat bloke over there was gonna take my guns."

Graham finished his cigar, tossing it to bounce along the bar. It landed in a pool of spilt whisky and the bar *whumped* into flames. "Best we be going now," Graham said. "We can catch up on the road."

As the bar burnt behind them, glowing orange and yellow in the night, the four rode out of town without looking back.

* * *

Shannon swung the ax, splitting the block of firewood in two. The sun was high in the sky above him and blazing hot. Sweat ran from the dark mop of brown hair atop his head. His bare chest and back glistened in the sunlight. Shannon bent over, setting another block of wood into place.

"I'll never in my life understand how you do it," Kira giggled as she came walking from the house with a pitcher of water and a cup in her hands. Shannon wiped the sweat from his face as best he could with the backside of his hand, taking in the sight of her. Her floral dress clung to her tightly in all the right places and hung slightly titled to one side revealing the soft skin of her shoulder. Her long blonde hair was pulled into a ponytail enhancing the sleekness of her neck and the angular features of her finely chiseled cheek bones. A smile stretched across full lips. She smelt of roses and store-bought perfume. She had turned twenty nine last month. They had celebrated with a midnight picnic atop the mountain, under the stars. But dang, she still bounced like an overactive and perky teenager.

Shannon met her smile with his own. "Do what?"

"Stay so blasted pale," she said, handing him the cup of water. It was cool and gone in only a few greedy gulps. Shannon gave her the mug to refill.

"I thought you liked how I look," he grinned.

"I'd like it better if you were on top of me again," she hinted, sitting the pitcher and cup in the grass. "But of course, you'd have to catch me first."

Kira lifted her dress, showing him some leg, then whirled about, running for the house. Shannon frowned, knowing how much work there was to be done today. He smiled as he watched her bare feet brushing through the green grass, tossed his ax aside. He leapt into a sprint, chasing after her.

From somewhere in the woods, a rifle cracked. The bullet caught him in the shoulder, tearing away a good chunk of meat. Its impact spun him around. A second shot rang out as another bullet ripped its way into his gut. Shannon could hear Kira screaming his name as she stood on the porch. His mouth opened to yell at her to get inside and lock the door but the third bullet smacked into the side of his head, rolling him off her knees where he had slumped onto the ground to land with his nose in the dirt. The last shot had been by far the most damaging. His vision blurred and the world seemed to spin as he tried to get up. A shiny, black boot caught him underneath his chin, snapping his head back, nearly breaking his neck. Shannon grabbed a hold on the leg it was attached to, jerking the man to the ground with him. He crawled onto the man, who struggled against Shannon's grip. Shannon sank his fingers into the man's throat, ripping it into a jagged mess of torn flesh. The man's blood exploded over him in blast of hot, red stickiness.

Shannon wondered who the man was and how many more like him were coming. A fresh wave of gunfire arose from inside the house. Shannon shook his head, trying to clear it. His shoulder was already mostly healed but his gut still hurt like hell and it was a fight to stay conscious. He could feel the bullet in his head grinding against the bone of his skull as his body tried to eject it. Shannon knew he wasn't thinking clearly. Then with the force of a cold dagger plunging into his heart, he realized Kira was in the house. He'd seen her take a bullet, splattering red over the front of her dress before two more men dragged her limp form inside. His perception of what was happening and his sense of time were all messed up, distorted and confused. Just a minute more, he prayed as the pain in his stomach subsided and he looked to see that the wound had healed as well. Another man in black, or was it three of them, came walking towards him. Shannon growled, low and sinister, at the stranger.

The man raised a colt at him and started firing before Shannon could leap. One bullet ripped through the flesh of his cheek. Another broke his nose before the final three formed a triangle of holes in his forehead. Then there was only blackness.

* * *

Shannon came to with a start, gulping air into his lungs. The sun was gone, replaced by the flickering light of the stars in the night sky above. He lay in the grass covered in his own congealed blood. "Kira!" he screamed, scrambling up and into a mad dash for the house. The door swayed partially open in the breeze as he leapt onto the porch. A trail of chestnut red, dried blood covered the steps, leading into the house.

Shannon staggered inside knowing what he was about to find. As dark as his thoughts were they did nothing to prepare him for what he saw. Kira's naked body was nailed to the wall. Large railroad spikes were driven through her hands and feet into the wood of the house, holding her several feet off the floor. Her head hung at an unnatural angle with the white of bone visible, poking from where her neck was bent. Her eyes were gone, leaving only empty sockets that seemed to stare at him in the dim starlight spilling in from the open doorway. Someone had cut her from her privates to her neck, emptying her out. Her organs and intestines lay in scattered piles below where she hung. Shannon fell to his knees, tears welling up in his eyes as he howled his fury in a raging cry that echoed throughout the valley.

* * *

When Shannon finished burying what remained of Kira, he stood in front of their home with a burning torch in his right hand. *Two Years,* he thought, *two years of perfect happiness and his future—gone.* Disgusted and hurting, he flung the torch into the house. He had doused the house in oil earlier. Flames exploded along the floor, running up the wall to ignite the ceiling. Shannon watched his life burning but had no tears left to shed. A familiar scent blew to him on the breeze. He turned to see four riders approaching in the distance. Whoever the men were that murdered Kira, they had taken his guns and shot his horses but that wouldn't stop him from finding them. These riders weren't those men. They were family. Family he had hoped he would never see again. The riders stopped just short of where he stood.

Graham cradled his hand against the wind as he struck a match on his thumb and lit a cigar. "Gotta tell you, Shannon, you're looking a mite rough these days."

Shannon's eyes flashed yellow as he flung himself at Graham. Zed leapt from his saddle to meet him. His younger brother caught him in mid-leap and the two of them tumbled into the grass. Shannon knew how fast Zed was so he wasted no time. He drove his fist into Zed's throat, crushing his windpipe. Zed coughed blood, gasping for breath, as Shannon left him where he lay. Yule came at him next. Shannon rolled his eyes, knowing this was going to hurt. Yule's massive fist slammed into him, shattering several of his ribs but that was what Shannon wanted. He let Yule close in so he could kick the giant in the side of his leg, breaking it at the knee. As Yule collapsed, Shannon caught him by the head. "Sorry, brother," he said then twisted Yule's thick neck hard until he heard the cracking noise of his spine snapping.

Graham had calmed his horse and retreated several yards. Shannon started for him again.

"Shannon!" Sarah yelled at him, stepping into his path. "Is this any way to treat greet your family?"

"Sarah, move out of my way," he warned her.

"I can't do that, Shannon, and you know it. I promised Mom I would take care of Graham. I can't let you hurt him."

"I don't intend to hurt him," Shannon snarled. "I intend to kill him."

Shannon rushed forward hoping to catch Sarah off guard. He swung at her, claws growing from the ends of his fingers. Sarah avoided his attack, meeting his nose with the flat of her palm. The bone of Shannon's nose separated into three pieces under his skin. Blood ran flowing over his lips and into his mouth but Sarah wasn't done. She caught his extended arm, flipping him over into the dirt on his back as she broke it. Shannon's skull was slammed back into the grass as he started to get up, her boot pinning him down as it met the soft flesh between his chin and his chest.

"No, Shannon!" she pleaded. "Stop this! Why do you want to hurt Graham so much?"

"They killed her Sarah," he whimpered, "They killed Kira."

Sarah took the heel of her boot off his throat. "Oh, Shannon," she said, "I am so sorry."

Shannon rolled over and wept as Zed and Yule joined Sarah, standing over him.

"Poor bastard," Zed commented to no one in particular. Yule only grunted.

"There's a stream not too far behind that inferno," Graham told them, still in his saddle. "Get him cleaned up and calmed down. We don't have time for this."

"He don't have no horse," Yule told Graham.

"Well, Zed can find him one," Graham snorted as he sauntered away on his horse, puffing on his cigar, to watch the burning house as its roof collapsed inward, causing sparks and glowing orange embers to dance in the wind.

* * *

Sarah and Yule sat on the bank of the stream as Shannon waded into its icy, moving waters to scrub at the blood and dirt caking his skin.

"Shannon," Sarah started, but he interrupted her.

"I'm not ready to talk about Kira yet, Sarah."

"Fine," she said, sounding hurt and angry. "Why did you go after Graham like that?"

Shannon snorted. "He's Graham. I'd wager my guns, if I still had them, that whatever he's up to had something to do with those men who murdered Kira and tried to kill me yesterday. He's trouble, Sarah. That's all he's ever been to any of us."

"He loves you like I do, Shannon, or we wouldn't be here." Sarah drew her colt, checking its chamber.

"No, Sarah. He needs me. There's a difference. We're all just soldiers to him, pawns to be used in whatever new game he's playing."

"Mom always said he was special," Yule added, removing his hat and staring at its threads like they contained all the secrets of the universe.

"Don't try to think, Yule," Shannon grumbled, "It's too painful to watch."

"Shannon!" Sarah snapped.

He sighed. "Sorry, Yule."

"It's all right," the big man smiled. "I may not be as sharp as Graham but I know you're hurting."

Yule's words stung him even though they weren't meant to. Shannon splashed to the bank. Sarah handed him a set of fresh clothes. "They're Zed's but I reckon beggars can't be choosers." She smiled at him.

Shannon shook the water from his body like a dog, then took the clothes, slipping them on as the others watched him. "You gonna tell me what Graham wants or let me die of old age waiting?"

"I think it's best you hear it from him given the circumstances." Sarah flipped the chamber of her colt shut.

"Well then," Shannon growled, "I guess it's time I went and found out."

Graham was waiting on him where the horses were tied at the edge of the woods. He lit another cigar as Shannon walked up to him.

"Do you always have to smoke?" Graham nodded at the house still burning nearby. "Shame about that. Bet it was a nice place."

"Don't push me, Graham. Sarah's not here to save you this time."

"You haven't changed," Graham snickered.

"Neither have you," Shannon said. "Why are you here, Graham? You know I'm done with the pack."

"Heck, Shannon, we all were but we're family. We have a responsibility. We're pure bloods. Do you know how rare that is these days?"

"I don't care. I'm tired of all the killing, Graham. I just wanted to live a normal life. Was that so much to ask?"

Graham waved his hand around at Shannon's property. "I didn't have anything to do with what happened here. I hope you know that."

"Why are you here?" Shannon asked again. "You know I'm not signing up for another of your private little wars."

Graham took a drag from his cigar, its end glowing orange in the darkness. "Samuel found it," he answered at last.

Shannon stared at him. "That's not possible."

"That was what I thought too but none the less, it's true. It's driven him mad, Shannon. He's building an army."

"An army?" Shannon spat into the dirt. "What for?"

"Don't know." Graham's voice took on a dark, serious edge. "But what I do know is that he's one of us. He's family and that means it's our job to put him down."

Shannon felt sick at the thought of putting a silver bullet in his brother's head. "Graham, are you sure?"

"Would I have come here if I wasn't?" Graham was insulted. "We all have our talents, Shannon. Samuel is mad and he has to be stopped."

At that moment, Zed zipped up to them leaving a trail of dust in his wake. "Ain't no horses around these parts. One of us is gonna be walking."

"Zed, you weigh next to nothing. Shannon can ride with you," Graham said.

Before Zed had the chance to protest, Shannon interrupted. "I haven't agreed to come with you yet."

"As I see it, you don't have a choice, Shannon. You're lying to yourself if you think different. All the blood Samuel's about to spill, that'll be on your hands, our hands. Stay here if you want but we're going after him."

"I hate you, Graham," Shannon growled.

"I get that a lot," Graham chuckled as Sarah and Yule joined them.

"You boys kiss and make up yet?" Sarah punched Graham in his shoulder, sending him staggering sideways.

"Ow!" he cried, "Did you really need to do that?" He rubbed at his arm then scooped his dropped cigar off the ground. It was nearly broken in half, the top half barely attached to the lower one. "Do you have any idea how much these cost?" he whined.

Sarah winked at Shannon. "I was just playing," she said, giving Graham a wicked grin. Shannon couldn't help but laugh. Zed and Yule joined in. Graham readjusted his hat and straightened his jacket. He stood tall, attempting to look tougher than he was and save some of his dignity. "Samuel is in Texas," he told them, "but he won't be there long."

"That's a three day ride," Yule's forehead creased as he spoke.

Zed shook his head. "Not for us, it ain't. As long as we can find fresh horses along the way, we can do it in one, two tops."

Sarah hopped onto her horse, slashing the rope that held it with a long fingernail. "See you there, boys!" she yelled over her shoulder at them, disappearing into the trees.

"Oh no she didn't!" Zed shouted, starting for his horse. Shannon's hand clamped onto his shoulder.

"Yes, she did and unless you're planning on running the whole way, you're gonna have to let it slide because I'm riding with you, remember?"

Zed cursed like a demon as the boys climbed into their saddles and rode after their sister.

Colonel Higgins pecked at the breakfast one of his aides had brought him. The eggs and coffee were both surprisingly good; a rare thing for a meal in the field. The truth of it, though, was that he simply had too much weighing on him to be as grateful as he should. His command tent did nothing to keep the smell of the dead from reaching his nostrils. When the wind blew just right he could smell the bodies rotting in the streets of Franklin. As hard as his men had worked for the last two days, there were still corpses waiting to be buried. His unit consisted of a grossly under-strengthened number of sixty men. They were all that could be spared for this assignment given the trouble stirring with the Mexicans to the south. Franklin's population was over five hundred, or at least it had been. Something, some force, had swept through the town, killing every single man, woman, and child in its path. The best count placed the number of mangled corpses at somewhere over three hundred and fifty. The rest of the folks were missing. It was possible they had fled whatever terror was unleashed in the town but his experience and gut told him they hadn't. There was no proof that those missing were dead, but he figured they were. It was his job to discover what had happened in this quiet hamlet and stop it from happening again. It was a job he took very seriously, however ill-equipped and unprepared he was to handle it. His men were scared. He could see it in their faces as he inspected their efforts in the afternoons. He didn't blame them. Not a random body here and there but all of the corpses appeared to have been killed by some kind of animal. Many seemed to have been gnawed on posthumously. Higgins knew the work of a wolf when he saw it and dang it, some of the wounds were so similar they rattled him to his core. Wolves seldom came into a town and he had never heard tell of a pack big and fast enough to kill hundreds of people, many of them armed, in a single attack. Nothing about this whole mess made any sort of sense. His men found numerous spent rifle cartridges all over the streets and men with their revolvers clutched so tightly in their cold hands they had to be pried free. But not a single body of an Indian, Mexican, or even a wolf. The people of Franklin looked to have put up one hell of a fight in certain sections of the town. He refused to believe that, despite their efforts, whoever did this got away without any losses.

Once again he went over the list of suspects in his mind, eliminating them one by one. Mexicans would have used guns. While Indian's tomahawks and knives could account for the mutilation of the corpses, the savages weren't cannibals. They took scalps as trophies sometimes. They didn't eat their enemies. Besides, there wasn't a single arrow or spear in the entire town to point the finger at them being the culprits of this massacre. And wolves, that was just insane. There was an answer somewhere, some vital clue he was overlooking, that would make all the pieces fit. He had to find it.

The flaps of his tent's door parted and Corporal Trantham poked his head inside. "Sir?" the corporal addressed him, "I am sorry to bother you but the men have found something we thought you would want to see."

Higgins scooted his unfinished plate of eggs away with a sad expression. "I'll be right there," he said guzzling the remainder of his coffee. He fastened his gun belt about his waist, taking a glance at his ragged and unkempt appearance in his small shaving mirror. His reflection bothered him, especially the new wrinkles he saw within it. One day this job would kill him. That was the one thing he was sure of.

From his unit's camp on the hill, Higgins rode into the town of Franklin, behind Corporal Trantham. A detachment of five cavalry men rode escort. The corporal led Higgins to the town's inn where two privates waited outside with rifles in their hands. They saluted as Higgins dismounted. "At ease, soldiers," he ordered.

"Upstairs, sir," the corporal glanced at the inn's second floor windows. Higgins stood in the street taking in the carnage and devastation around them before heading inside.

One of the guest rooms upstairs was the scene of what must have been a furious battle. Its door, now shattered into fragments of jagged wood littering the floor, had been locked and barricaded for all the good it had done the poor souls in the room. Bullet holes riddled the walls and dried blood tainted everything a wretched shade of brown. Higgins nearly slipped on the shell casings beyond the broken door. There were so many he couldn't count them all. Three bodies were present. One was a man in a long coat with his throat torn to shreds. Something about him told Higgins the man was a professional killer who was passing through town and got caught in the middle of whatever happened here. Another of the bodies was a whore. She lay near the window with a naked man on top of her. It was this third corpse that demanded his attention. The man's lips and mouth were smeared with dried blood and his right hand was closed over the whore's throat. Deep gashes in the whore's skin that looked like claw marks ended where his had rested on her. A small knife protruded from the backside of the naked man's neck where Higgins guessed the whore had planted it as she died. Higgins scowled at the corporal.

"Don't you think it's odd that he's naked, sir?" Trantham asked.

Higgins shrugged. "For your sake, Corporal, I hope there's more to this than what I am currently seeing."

Corporal Trantham knelt beside the naked man, parting the blue lips with his fingers to show Higgins the teeth. Higgins crossed himself as he saw them. They were long and curved like an animal's.

"What does this mean, sir?" Trantham asked.

Higgins moved closer to the corpse and jerked the small knife from the naked man's spine, examining the blade in the sunlight coming through the room's open window. It was silver. The gears of his mind began to turn, assembling the pieces of Franklin's mystery. They gave him an answer that sent a shiver coursing through him and made him doubt his sanity. "It means," Higgins answered, "either I've lost my mind or we're in for the fights of lives if we catch the crowd that did all this."

* * *

The people of Yarbrough stared as the family rode into their little town. Shannon could see the mingled looks of fear and curiosity on their faces. He and the others brought their horses to a halt outside the town's saloon which also served as its inn.

"I could use a stiff drink," Yule announced.

"Do what you want," Graham nodded, "just remember we're not staying. Shannon, you and Sarah go with him and try to keep him out of trouble."

"What about you?" Shannon asked.

"Someone's got to get us new horses. We've pushed these too hard already."

"I want a drink too," Zed complained.

"Forget it. You're with me," Graham ordered as Yule tied up their exhausted mounts and the family went their separate ways.

Even in her loose gunfighter attire, Sarah turned more than a few heads as she led Shannon and Yule into the saloon. Shannon wondered if Yule was really the one Graham wanted him to keep an eye on. Sarah strolled up to the bar, slapping two dollars in front of the startled bartender. "Whisky, and keep it coming."

The bartender was a middle-aged man with a gray speckled beard. "Ma'am," he said with sincere concern in his voice, "are you sure that's a good idea?"

Shannon grabbed her wrist below the bar as hand moved towards what he assumed was some kind of weapon tucked inside of her coat.

"It's for us," he nodded at Yule.

The bartender relaxed, beaming at them. "Pick a table if you want and I'll have one of the girls bring you a bottle."

"Thank you," Shannon said, dragging Sarah gently away from the bar.

"I wasn't going to kill him," she whispered angrily. "You shouldn't have stopped me. Having only one ear might have made him more attractive. Some ladies really like scars."

"What would you know about scars?" Shannon laughed as the trio took a seat at a table in the rear of the establishment.

"You owe me one," Sarah told him. Shannon knew she would collect someday, too.

A serving girl arrived with their drinks. Sarah snatched the bottle of whisky from the tray, chugging half of it before slamming its bottom onto the table. The girl gasped, startled by Sarah's boorish behavior.

"What you waiting for, honey?" Sarah sloshed what remained of the whisky around inside the bottle. "I ain't about to tip you."

The girl fled towards the bar.

"Sarah, you don't have anything to prove," Shannon said,. "There's no reason to act like this. Remember we're supposed to be blending in."

Sarah stuck out her tongue at him.

Shannon met her eyes. "Kira really liked you," he said sadly.

Sarah looked like he'd just slapped her in the face. Her expression shifted from mocking anger to one of pity. "I don't get it, Shannon. What do you see in *them?* Humans are so frail."

"They're exactly like us in all the ways that matter, Sarah. Exactly. They have families, dreams, and they love. Graham can put them down and call them inferior all he wants but that doesn't make it true. That's why I left. I'm tired of pointless power games and getting blood on my hands. I want more out of life than that."

"I know," she admitted. "I do too. The three years we were apart, I was living in Tibet. I went there searching for answers but only found more questions. I'm almost beginning to believe that peace is a make believe word that folks throw around to gave them hope."

Shannon noticed Yule was watching the two of them with a confused frown. He patted one of his brother's thick arms. "What about you, Yule? What do you want in this life?"

"Not to die," Yule answered, taking the bottle of whisky Sarah held and finishing it.

Shannon and Sarah laughed at his simple but true answer.

"I think we can all agree on that, Yule," Shannon nodded.

Yule lit up like a kid, happy to have contributed to the conversation.

"So you want love, I want peace, and all of us want to be immortal?" Sarah chuckled darkly, "Guess that means we're all screwed huh?"

The serving girl returned, placing two more bottles of whisky and three shot glasses in front of them. Yule was laughing, shaking the whole table, but Shannon kept quiet.

"I don't know," he said, "Those first two might be possible if we try hard enough. I can vouch that love is real at least." His expression was melancholy and brooding. "I can promise you when I find the ones that took Kira from me, they will be begging me to send them to Hell before I'm done with them."

"Well, what have we here?" A Mexican man in a poncho asked as he and five other rough and tumble men encircled their table. His gaze was fixed on Sarah, lingering far too long on her breasts before he looked over at Shannon and Yule.

So much for staying out of trouble, Shannon thought as the Mexican leaned over Sarah.

"You've got bad taste in men, Chica. Why don't you come share a drink with some real hombres?"

Shannon gave Yule a look that suggested the big man to keep his cool and let Sarah handle this. Yule glared at the Mexican but stayed in his chair.

"You guess my age and I'll come with you." Sarah batted her eyelashes at the men. "Get it wrong and I *will* kill you where you stand. How does that sound to you?"

"Why you gotta go and be like that, Chica?" The Mexican turned to his friends. "I think she just insulted me, amigos. What do you think?"

A murmur of agreement rippled through the gang. The Mexican leaned over Sarah again. Shannon could smell his foul breath from where he sat across the table.

"I think I should just take what I want," he whispered to Sarah, not realizing Shannon and Yule could hear him too.

"I'm waiting on your guess if you're man enough to play," Sarah said loudly, making sure the other men heard her challenge.

With a sneer on his face, the Mexican's eyes roamed over her. "You're twenty two if you're a day."

"Wrong," Sarah grinned. "I'm seventy four." She grabbed him by his hair and smashed his mouth into the side of the table. She released him as he spat out blood and pieces of broken teeth. Sarah got to her feet, facing the others. "You're lucky. I'm in a generous mood today so I'll let you all live if you leave now. I ain't telling you twice."

Shannon lowered his head into his hands. Sarah, for all her good intent, had just put the men into a position where they had to fight. No man could back away from a woman like her in public and live it down, no matter how tough a show Sarah put on.

"Fff-ill F-her!" the Mexican howled as the men went for their guns.

Shannon nudged Yule, telling the big man to step in. At least that way, some of them might make it out of the saloon alive. Yule leapt up, throwing the table like a discus into the men. Only a two of them managed to get off a couple shots before the table sent them all tumbling. Both shots were wild, missing the family entirely.

"Yule!" Sarah raged at the giant. "Stay out of this!"

The men were clamoring to their feet as Sarah tore into them. She lifted one by his throat, effortlessly, with a single hand above her head. His eyes were wide with terror as her other hand drew one of the colts holstered underneath her duster, blowing a hole in one of his friends. Sarah jerked the man dangling above her closer and bit his nose, tearing it from his face with her teeth. She spat it from her red-smeared lips at the rest of the men. As they screamed from the sight of their nose-less amigo, Sarah flung him across the room. One of the men leveled a revolver at her head, taking aim, but before he could pull the trigger, Sarah flung a small metal star at him. It spun through the air, its three blades whirling, to bury itself in his forehead. As his body toppled over, the others lost what courage they had left, running for the saloon's door. Sarah turned her back on them. "Yule, fix the table please," she ordered, "And barkeep, we're going to need some more whiskey!"

Shannon watched her, shaking his head, a wide smile on his lips.

* * *

Graham and Zed headed straight for the stables on the town's outskirts. Zed bounced along like he was on the verge of exploding from the energy coursing in his veins. "Graham, it's kind of weird, all of us together again, ain't it?"

"It's how things are meant to be. If we'd stayed together, maybe we wouldn't be on the way to kill our brother."

"It wasn't your fault, Graham. Shannon and Samuel weren't about to stay. They had plans of their own and needed more than the pack could give them. Yule and I only left because Sarah did. Didn't seem much point in hanging around after that."

Zed watched the emotions flicking over Graham's face. "Wait a second, you blame Shannon for Samuel, don't you?"

"Shannon was the first to leave the pack," Graham commented without giving a real answer. Then he changed the subject. "You're a lot smarter than you act, Zed. Why did you stay with Yule even after the two of you took off?"

"He needed someone, Graham. You know that. For all his strength, he's just a big kid. He'd be dead right now if I hadn't."

Graham stopped, turning to Zed. "The one thing that's always troubled me about you, Zed, is that you underestimate yourself. You're so much more than you think you are."

Zed didn't know what to say. Praise from Graham was about as expected as frogs falling from the sky on a sunny afternoon. Zed spotted the man who looked to run the stable, leading a horse into its stall from the corral. He decided it best to ignore Graham's compliment. "Come on," he told Graham, leading his brother on across the street. The man must have seen them coming. He waved at them.

"Good afternoon, gentlemen."

"Good afternoon," Graham nodded, tipping his hat at the man.

Zed felt his stomach tighten and his head grow lighter on his shoulders. All he wanted to do was run as far away as he could, but he forced himself to shake the feeling off. "You're doing the *thing*, aren't you?" he whispered to Graham. "I hate it when you do the thing."

"How much for five horses?" Graham asked.

The man twitched with primal fear as he spoke. "Whatever you think is fair, mister."

Graham flipped a few bills from the roll he carried in his jacket pocket, giving them to the man. "You can go now. We'll pick them ourselves."

The stable owner, clearly relieved to get away from Graham, scurried away to tend to one of the horses still outside.

"How much did you pay him?" Zed asked.

"More than I should have. Shannon must be rubbing off on me." Graham pretended to shudder.

Graham and Zed led the horses to the saloon.

"Wait here," Graham said. "I'll fetch the others."

Zed tied up the horses and paced around, kicking rocks with the tip of his boot. He thought about what Graham said. Was he really more than he was allowing himself to be?

A group of ten men, led by a Mexican with a blood-smeared mouth, came up the street towards the saloon. Zed stepped up to meet them. "What's the hurry, amigos?"

"It's no concern of yours," snapped a tall, bearded man with a silver star pinned to the breast of his coat.

Zed blocked the group's path. "Oh, I think it is." His hands brushed back the sides of his duster to show the hilts of his custom made Colts. The group of men stopped, most of them laughing so loud Zed wanted to rip out their tongues.

"Son," the man with the badge said. "You don't want to do this."

One of the others slapped the sheriff's shoulder. "If the little runt wants to have a go at us, we can all chip in to buy him a coffin. Bet one his size is pretty cheap."

The men continued to roar with laughter.

"What's the matter?" Zed taunted them. "You gents afraid of me?"

"Watch it, runt!" one of the men yelled.

"Please, kid," the sheriff begged. "Don't do this. You're outgunned and too young to throw your life away like this."

"Thanks, Sheriff," Zed grinned, "for that, I'll let you live but I ain't no kid."

"To Hell with this," one of the men said, going for his pistol.

A chorus of rapid gunfire thundered in the street. Zed watched the stunned sheriff look to his right, then to his left. All the other men lay dead or twitching in the dirt. Not a single one had got their gun clear of their holster. Zed stood in the center of the street, twirling his Colts so fast on his fingers they made a whirring noise. He ended his display, flipping the pistols around into the holsters on his hips.

"Told you I would let you live, Sheriff, but now I suggest," Zed flicked his head to the side, "you run."

The sheriff didn't have to be told twice. Zed was watching him high-tail it towards the edge of town as the rest of the family emerged from the saloon. Several of the men he'd shot were still moaning as they died.

"Zed!" Shannon and Graham growled at the same time. Zed removed his hat, scratching at his head.

"Don't blame me, mates. They were the ones who had size issues."

"Later," Graham said, pointing a finger at him, "We'll be having a discussion about what keeping a low profile means."

As the family saddled their horses, Sarah gave Zed a quick peck on his cheek. "I know what that's like," she whispered. Zed smiled.

* * *

Colonel Higgins got some strange stares from his officers when he ordered them to gather all the silver in Franklin and boil it down into bullets. None of them challenged his orders though. Either they weren't brave enough to confront him or somewhere deep inside, they suspected the same thing he did. When you ruled out everything that was possible, sometimes the impossible was the only answer that made any sense. Higgins wanted to send some men to bring reinforcements but that would mean giving an explanation as to why they were needed. Instead he sent for Father Jericho. Jericho was something of a legend in these parts for his exorcisms. The young priest was said to be a few cards short of a full deck. He roamed Texas hunting for demons and monsters that he fully believed were real even after the church had excommunicated him for his wild ideas. Higgins was desperate, grasping at straws, but he needed someone he could share his beliefs with and the priest fit the bill. If he was, by the grace of God, wrong about what happened in Franklin, he might be able to keep his commission if the priest talked. No one would take the priest's word over his own.

Higgins spent most of his time searching for the answer to another very important question: How many? How many of the creatures would it have taken to kill this whole town and do so much damage so quickly? Another question haunted him as well: Why? If the monsters were real, why had he never heard of an attack like this before?

As the sun began to sink behind the hills, he was forced to abandon his search for answers and return to his unit's camp. During the ride back, he couldn't help but keep an eye on the bushes his party passed, waiting for red-smeared, razored teeth to spring at him from the shadows. Every time he heard the howl of a wolf in the distance, he nearly wet himself.

Father Jericho was waiting for him in his tent when he arrived. The priest was dressed in filthy and well-worn clothes that had seen better days. Even his clerical collar was tainted brown from wear. He was lean with the appearance of a beggar. Higgins placed Father Jericho's age at somewhere in his late twenties. He clutched a tattered Bible in his hands but what really caught Higgins' attention were the weapons on the priest's belt. A gleaming, silver revolver was holstered on his right hip and a well kept Tomahawk dangled from the other side.

"Colonel Higgins," the priest extended a hand. Higgins shook it. As Higgins met Father Jericho's eyes, he saw a hardness in them that reminded him of the best soldiers he'd known in his career.

"Thank you for coming, Father." Higgins took a seat at his makeshift desk, offering Jericho the edge of his sleeping cot as a chair.

"It's not often armed soldiers march into my camp during the wee hours of the morning to request my presence."

"Have you heard what's happened here in Franklin?"

"Rumors, nothing more. As it happens, I was traveling here myself when your men found me."

"Why?" Higgins asked.

"Surely you know the answer to that or you wouldn't have sent for me." Jericho scratched at the stubble on his cheeks. "I saw the town as your men escorted me to your camp. At a distance, yes, but enough to know you have a dangerous and powerful enemy."

Higgins chuckled, pouring himself a shot of whiskey. "Do you drink, Father?"

Father Jericho shook his head.

"Then I hope you will forgive me but I really need one right now."

"What kind?" Father Jericho asked.

"What do you mean?" Higgins raised an eyebrow at the priest.

"All manner of demons and abominations walk this Earth, Colonel. What kind are we facing here?"

Higgins swallowed his shot, finding the courage to say the word out loud for the first time. "Werewolves, Father. Tell me everything you know about werewolves."

Father Jericho smiled, placing his hands atop his Bible.

* * *

Shannon thought about Kira as the family pressed southward. The hole in his heart from her loss ached like nothing he'd ever known. He could still feel the touch of her fingertips tracing over his chest, smell her hair, and taste her lips on his. He should be on the trail of the men who murdered her and he swore he would be as soon as Samuel was dealt with. Of the whole family, Samuel was the only one who had really understood when he'd left the pack. Graham might be the smartest of them but Samuel was the most cunning. Even with all of the family together again, with Graham leading them, finding Samuel wouldn't be an easy thing unless he wanted to be found. Each of the family possessed their own gift. Zed could move like a Cheetah. Yule was so strong he could rip into a steel vault with his bare hands. Sarah was a natural born killer, as skilled as Athena would be if the Goddess descended to Earth wielding a six-gun. Graham played with emotions and fought his battles with words and wit. Samuel was one with the darkness. The shadows were his friends and his minions. The occult called to Samuel like a flame to a moth. If Graham was telling the truth, Samuel was a danger that couldn't be ignored and worse, he was their responsibility. Who else could stand against him and have even a snowball's chance in Hell of stopping him? Like Graham, Samuel believed the humans were inferior and merely meat. He hated them with a passion that burnt as bright as the moon on a starless night. The ancient laws binding their kind meant nothing to him even in his youth.

"You're thinking too much," Zed said, riding up beside him. "Not that I mind after those years with only Yule for company but you've got that 'we're screwed' scent about you. Ease up, Shannon. Life's too short, even for us, to waste it."

"Why, Zed, when did you become a philosopher?"

"I'm serious, mate. Hope is the key to happiness, without it there's not much to living. Honor Kira by living. She'd appreciate that a good sight more than you spilling more blood in her name. We've got enough of that ahead with Samuel I reckon anyway. He ain't gonna let us walk up to him and end it."

Shannon frowned at Zed.

"If we live through this mess, I'll wager one day you'll find that kind of love again." Zed spurred his horse, galloping ahead as he laughed. "Even if it is Sarah."

Shannon failed to find the humor in Zed's joke.

"Did I hear my name?" Sarah asked, rising up from behind him.

Aw crap, Shannon thought, flashing her a fake smile. "Just Zed being Zed," he told her, trying to play off the growing redness on his cheeks.

"I heard him, ya know?"

"Sarah, I. . ."

"I'm not stupid, Shannon. I know you're too human in your ways to even. . ." her voice trailed off as she glanced up at the night sky. "It won't be long until the moon is full."

"No," Shannon agreed. "I reckon not."

* * *

Samuel darted through the trees, zigging one way, zagging another. A small, white rabbit was trying hard to elude him. Samuel was playing with it. The nostrils on the end of his snout flared as he savored its scent of fear. The rabbit knew it was dead. It was only attempting to buy a few more precious moments of life. It poured on the speed, curving around a tree. Samuel's four legs carried him around the tree's other side to meet the rabbit there. His teeth closed on its neck, crushing the bones inside it with his powerful jaws. Hot blood flooded his mouth, bathing his tongue. Samuel enjoyed his meal in the moonlight, picking the rabbit's bones clean. When he was done, he howled his victory at the sky above. He knew they were coming, the whole family, together again. His agents reported that they were in Texas and drawing ever closer. Part of him was thrilled at the challenge they would bring. Humans, like the rabbit, were far too easy prey. They offered little sport to one such as him. He had to admit he was surprised to hear Shannon was with the others. Shannon wasn't a killer. Samuel hoped that at least one of the others would listen to reason and come to see the world as he did, but he doubted it. Not even Graham had the stomach for what he had planned. Shannon would certainly stand against him. He loved the humans so much it sickened Samuel and made him ashamed to call him blood. Samuel wasn't truly worried about his family. Not even they could stop him, but the confrontation would most certainly be amusing. He loosed a final howl and ran from the woods to the clearing where his men waited. His joints popped, his muscles tearing apart and reforming as the hair covering his body receded into his skin. In a matter of seconds, a naked man crouched where there once had been a wolf. Blood stained his lips, chin and cheeks.

Harold handed him a hooded, black robe as Ed and Kevin watched. Samuel shrugged on the robe, cleaning his lips on its sleeve.

"You have fun, boss?" Ed asked.

Samuel ignored the question, responding with one of his own: "Any further word of my family's exact whereabouts?"

"Not since they left Yarbrough, boss," Kevin answered.

"We're ready to move on the town of Seger, though. The fellers are chomping at the bit to let loose again."

"Well done." Samuel picked a piece of rabbit hide from his teeth. "Remember, take only those who show the most potential."

"And the others?" Harold bared his yellow, tobacco stained teeth. "Same as last time?"

"Yes," Samuel waved a hand dismissively. "Leave no survivors. Let the humans' blood run like a river through the streets."

"You coming along this time, boss?" Ed asked.

Samuel shook his head, raising his left hand with his fingers spread apart. Bright blue energy crackled and danced over his palm and between them. "As tempting as the thought of doing so may be, alas, I have other business to attend to."

* * *

Colonel Higgins tried to keep a straight face as Father Jericho swooned, swaying back and forth on his feet, in the rays of the early morning sun. In truth, Higgins didn't know if he should laugh or cry. The priest hummed a continuous note that was beginning to grate on his nerves. As if having only Father Jericho's crazy methods to guide him and his men wasn't bad enough, he was trusting the success of his mission, the lives of his men, and his career to this lunatic.

The priest's eyes snapped open and he screamed a word in an Indian tongue Higgins didn't understand..

"Well?" Higgins asked as Father Jericho staggered towards him. "You want to tell me what in the heck you were just doing?"

"It's called a spirit trance, Colonel."

"And God approves of you doing that?"

"The Indians believe such methods allow their totem animals to guide them in life. In reality, such a state enhances one's own perceptions and brings one closer to God to better hear his will. He made the human mind to be capable of far more than most know or even comprehend."

"I don't remember that being in the Bible," Higgins pointed out.

Father Jericho scowled at him.

"So, did you find the monsters?"

"No, Colonel, but I did find their trail. They're headed south to Seger. I'd stake my life on that fact. That taint of their evil pulses like a burning flame in the darkness."

"All right," Higgins said. "You better be right about this, Father. I don't want any more innocent blood spilled by those things." Higgins also didn't want to be court-martialed. The message he had sent to his superiors was a lie. He had said that a rogue band of savages were responsible for the Franklin massacre and that he was in pursuit, hoping to catch them before they reached the Mexican border. Higgins needed to find the monsters to save his own hide as much as the lives of whatever poor folks the beasts might come across before he caught them.

"You're not a man of faith, are you, Colonel?" Father Jericho asked him as Higgins handed him a canteen of water.

"Oh, I have plenty of faith, Father. Faith in a good strong horse, the bullets in my pistol, and in this country we live in."

"Surely you must have faith in more than those things or you wouldn't be putting such trust in me."

"Don't read too much into things, Father," Higgins laughed. "I'm desperate."

The rest of the men were still waiting in their saddles as the two of them climbed onto their horses.

"We will never catch them before they reach Seger," Father Jericho said.

Higgins knew the priest was right about that but he gave the signal for his men to move out, spurring his horse into motion. "We'll see about that, Father!" he shouted. "But even if we don't, those things are still going to pay!"

Graham gnawed at the nail of his left ring finger. Sarah was bathing in the stream where the family had stopped for breakfast. Zed sat beside the fire, where Shannon was warming beans, sipping on a cup of coffee. Yule stood on the bank of the stream pointlessly watching over Sarah. She didn't need his protection any more than Zed needed coffee. They had pressed on through the night. Their eyesight was far better than a normal man's but even they had to eat.

Graham was happy they were all together again. During the time they had been apart his life just had not been the same. He had served time as an officer in the army, barking orders from the relative safety of his command tent, well behind the lines. He'd run a publishing house in New York that specialized in "off color" fiction such as ghost stories and fantastic tales of the supernatural. Most of that time he'd spent drifting from town to town, amassing a fortune from gambling. He owned numerous saloons, brothels, and restaurants all across the country. Graham had also developed a network of informants and information traders that he relied upon heavily at times like this, but to be truthful, none of it was close to the excitement of the old days when the pack was known as the best group of guns for hire in the West. Those days were gone, lost in the sands of time, but watching the others now was almost enough to give him hope they could be a unit again after Samuel had been dealt with. Graham frowned. He and Samuel had never seen eye to eye but up until Shannon's heart had led him astray, Samuel was the only one of his family that challenged him. Though they had never came to blows, because that wasn't their way, their arguments over how the pack should handle itself and what jobs they should take were some of the high points of those adventures. Samuel's intellect rivaled his own in some areas and exceeded it in others though he would never admit that to any of his family.

While Graham was a self-taught scholar of the world, well read in the classics and versed in the dynamics of modern engineering, Samuel had hungered for a different kind of knowledge, a dark and forbidden kind—the magic of the days of old before man rose to power over the world. As a child, Samuel loved the tales their mother had told them of her homeland far to the north. Graham enjoyed these stories as nothing more than entertainment but Samuel committed them to memory, dissecting each for the kernels of truth that lay within them. By the time they were teenagers, Samuel was determined to prove to Graham that magic was real. As the years passed, Samuel raided monasteries, libraries, and even began to hunt famous occultists and shamans to accumulate their knowledge. Samuel claimed he conversed with demons and beings from far beyond the world that Graham knew. Neither Shannon nor any of the others suspected that Samuel sought much more than simple psychological power. Graham, however, came to realize more and more what drove Samuel. Their parents were murdered by hunters sent by the church in Europe. Samuel's hatred of the church and all humans consumed him and continued to grow as he plotted his vengeance and sought the means to deliver it upon humanity as a whole. Graham watched Samuel's skill in the dark arts go from parlor tricks, for which he was of course mocked, to spells that made even him a believer. He'd once seen Samuel drain the soul of a human, leaving only a withered and crumpled husk of a body in place of a strong and vital man in his twenties.

There was a singular entity that caught Samuel's interest above all others. The stories told by their mother said that it dwelt in the lands to the north, and when Shannon found the courage to leave the pack, Samuel followed in his wake because he truly believed that if he could find this spirit, he'd capture it and take its power for himself. Sarah, Zed, and Yule were clueless in regard to Samuel's goal but like himself, Shannon knew.

Like Samuel, he had never been normal. Graham always poked fun at Shannon, saying that he had the soul of a human. Shannon was a hopeless romantic with delusions fueled by love and hope. He adopted humanity's morals and lived by them as much as his nature would permit. Their heritage wasn't the curse Shannon thought it to be. It was something special, setting them apart and above humanity. The primal urges that haunted Shannon were no more evil than a storm that spread wildfires on the plains or a twister that swept away the works of man. They were simply part of the natural order of this world, like all else.

"Graham!" Zed called to him. "Stop brooding and come get some coffee."

Graham frowned but joined his brothers at the fire. He took the cup of steaming hot, black liquid Zed had concocted and labeled coffee. Taking a sip from the cup, he grimaced. "Are you trying to kill me or turn me into you?" Graham teased, trying to lighten his own mood.

Zed laughed. Graham noticed Shannon shoveling in a spoonful of beans.

"Still slumming it, I see. If you're going to eat like the humans instead of hunting your food out here in the wild, you could have packed something more tasteful than beans."

"Don't knock them until you've tried them," Shannon shot back at him.

"I think I will pass on that offer." Graham turned to see Sarah, her hair dripping wet, with her hats in her hands, returning from the steam. Yule lumbered along behind her.

"You feel better?" he asked.

"Much," Sarah smiled. "You boys should really learn to bathe more often. It'll do wonders for you with the women folk."

"The horses are rested," Yule announced in his usual loud and rumbling voice.

"Finish your beans, little brother," Graham instructed Shannon. "Samuel is waiting on us."

Zed drained the last of his coffee. "You really think he knows we're coming for him?"

"He knows," Graham nodded. "You can bet on that. Samuel's a lot of things but a fool isn't one of them."

* * *

Sheriff Mark Johnson strolled along Seger's main street, saying good morning and tipping his hat to the folks he passed. He was in a good mood today. Last night, Kira had finally said yes. After years of courting her, they were going to get married. Something like that deserved celebrating so he was headed to Moe's for the biggest breakfast of his life.

Old man Henry sat outside his general store.

"Morning, Hank," Mark beamed at him.

The old man preferred to be called Hank instead of Mr. Henry. Said he wasn't no mister and never would be. Hank spat a mouthful of brown, slimy tobacco juice into a jar beside him, wiping his lips on the sleeve of his shirt.

"Morning, Sheriff. You look kind of chipper for this early."

"Ain't no reason not to be," Mark smiled.

The old man snorted. "Give it a couple of years, boy, and I reckon you'll think different."

"What?" Mark asked, then he realized Hank must somehow know already about his engagement. "Dang, news in this town travels fast. Don't reckon I'll ever get used to that."

"Maybe if'n you'd stayed in the big city," the old man grumbled.

Mark shook his head. "You better be careful Hank or I will start believing you're as cranky as folks say you are."

"It's a free country. Believe what you like but if you ain't figured that much out by now, what living here for three years now, you better have Doc Bryson take a look at your head."

Mark flashed him a grin and continued on up the street. Vincent was waiting outside the restaurant as he arrived.

"Figured you'd be here this morning."

Dang, does everyone already know? Mark wondered. Mark knew his deputy well enough to know that something was wrong. "What's the problem, Vincent?"

"I slept in the jail yesterday evening."

"Marlene still on you about gambling?"

Vincent nodded, wringing his hat in his hands. "Threatened to split my head open if I came home. You know how she gets."

"Sorry to hear about that."

"Anyhow, around three o'clock in the morning, there's this pounding on the door. Thought the feller was gonna tear it down. He was screaming about monsters in the hills and how they were coming for us. He was so torn up, I had to knock him out to get him to calm any. Got him locked up for the time being. He don't seem right so I figured I better fetch you. Didn't know what else to do. Doc Bryson is still out of town, gone to check on Mr. Hendrickson's wife and her heart condition up at their farm."

Mark sighed, casting a longing look at the tables inside Moe's through the large front window. "Right then," he agreed. "Let's go have a talk with this feller and see what all the ruckus is about."

Several more folks stopped them on their way to the jail to congratulate Mark or tease him about his engagement. All he could think about was the heaping plate of eggs and sausage he was missing.

The man in the cell was rough looking. Mark pegged him at once as being a stage driver. He'd passed through town before on his route and had never made any trouble. Mark didn't see any signs that he'd been drinking. Picking up a chair, Mark placed it facing into the cell and took a seat as the stage driver watched him. "My deputy here tells me you got out of hand last night, nearly scared him to death trying to get in here. Wanna tell me why a grown man would try to break into a jail during the middle of the night, yelling about monsters?"

"You gonna knock me on my arse like he did if I do?" the stage driver asked, cocking his head at Vincent and rubbing at a large, purple bruise covering the right side of his jaw.

"Don't plan on it, anyways," Mark answered, glancing at Vincent, wondering why the deputy couldn't have been some gentler with this man. If he'd broken the man's jaw, they'd never be having this conversation, least not until the Doc got back into town and fixed it.

"Sheriff, my name is Lionel Jenkins. I drive the stage that comes through these here parts."

"I know who you are, Mr. Jenkins," Mark said. "That ain't what I asked."

"I was on my way here yesterday. Robert was riding shotgun like always. Had two passengers in the coach. One minute, everything was dandy, the next we were all fighting for our lives. These three. . . things, big hairy creatures stronger than angry bears, came from nowhere and jumped us." Lionel shuddered as he told his tale. "They ripped Robert in half. I ain't exaggerating. Two of them grabbed him and yanked him apart right down the middle. He managed to shoot one of them before they got him, point blank with a double barrel. The thing staggered but that was it. I know he hit it, Sheriff. I saw its blood splatter and the hole in its chest but it just kept on coming like nothing had happened. Anyway, the other one that didn't go after Robert tore the door off the side of the coach and tossed it away like it weren't nothing but kindling. By that time, I was full out sprinting for the trees. I heard the passengers screaming like they were dying.

"All I had was my Colt and I knew if Robert's shotgun didn't stop them things, my gun sure wasn't about to. Reckon they must have forgot about me in their excitement when they discovered one of the passengers was a fine, young woman from out east somewhere. Ain't never heard nothing crying like she was doing but I . . . I was too scared to try to help her. I kept right on running. That's when I saw the rest of them. There were six more of the things, walking about on two legs, with this group of, I guess, four or five dozen armed men. None of them had horses. They was just out there like they was waiting on something. But that ain't the worst of it as far as you're concerned, Sheriff. I heard one of them say they was coming here. This was the only town I could make it to on foot so I came on, just praying I would beat 'em here. From what I saw them do to Robert and listening to how they went at that young girl, I figured you deserved to be warned that they was on their way."

Mark stared at Lionel for a long time. His gut told him the stage driver was telling the truth but the man's story was pure craziness. "Thank you for that," Mark said at last. "You wait here a minute. Vincent and I will see about sorting this mess out and talk about letting you go."

Mark got up, motioning for Vincent to follow him outside of the jailhouse. Lionel leapt to his feet in the cell, grabbing the bars with both his hands. "You gotta believe me, Sheriff Johnson! I ain't lying and I ain't been drinking either. It's the truth. You gotta let me out before they get here!"

Mark and Vincent stepped into the street, shutting the heavy, wooden door to the jail and silencing the rest of Lionel's cries.

"I can see why you came and got me," Mark admitted. "That son of a gun is off his rocker."

"Don't I know it?" Vincent agreed. "What are we gonna do with him?"

"He ain't broke no laws that we know of yet but I ain't too keen on letting him loose. No telling what a man like that might do next." Mark thought for a moment. "The first thing we're gonna do is go have a look at that trail in the hills ourselves."

"You mean I am, don't ya?" Vincent frowned.

"Nice of you offer," Mark grinned. "Don't waste no time doing it. I want you back here as soon as you can be."

"I'll head straight there."

"Round up Nathan and take him with you," Mark laughed, slapping Vincent on his shoulder, "I'd be plum heart broke if the monsters got you."

* * *

Vincent found Nathan sleeping off a rough night in one of the saloons upper rooms. It took emptying the water from the wash bowl over his hair to wake him. "Ain't no proper conduct for a man of the law," Vincent grumbled as he dragged Nathan down the stairs. Several of the showgirls and whores giggled at them.

"Bye, girls," Nathan groggily waved. Then to Vincent: "Ah come on. Do you have to be so loud? My skull feels like a mule kicked it."

"Ought to be ashamed," Vincent grumbled on as they mounted up and rode northward. It took two hours to reach the place in the stage's route where Lionel claimed the attack had taken place.

"I'll be. . ." Vincent swore as they came upon the overturned stage. The horses were dead. Whatever killed them did a quick job of it, slashing their throats into tatters of exposed, red meat. One of the stage's doors lay across the road from it in the dirt. There was blood everywhere and a buzzard sat atop the corpse of a naked woman, pecking at one of her eye sockets. Vincent saw Nathan cross himself. He'd told Nathan Lionel's story on the ride.

Vincent hopped to the ground for a better look.

"Maybe that crazy feller ain't so crazy," Nathan said quietly. "I think we should get out of here, Vincent."

Vincent dropped to his knees and vomited in the dust as he saw the woman closer. Her groin was torn so wide her privates were a gaping hole you could slide a small cannon ball into. Her face was contorted into an expression of pain mixed with utter terror. Deep grooves creased her naked flesh like the claw marks of a bear.

"Uh, Vincent, I think I see the man who was supposed to be riding shotgun. Part of him anyway."

Vincent righted himself, walking back to his horse. "Forget him. We've seen what he came to see." He jerked his Winchester from the holster on the side of his horse's saddle and kept it in his hand as he mounted.

"What do you reckon did this?" Nathan asked. "I don't see no tracks."

"Whatever it was it could be watching us," Vincent cautioned the younger deputy. "You be ready, boy. From those horses, I'd say whatever did this is so dang fast, we won't even see it coming."

"Shouldn't we bury her or something?"

"Dead's dead. You wanna stick around and do it, you'll be by yourself." Vincent turned his horse and screamed "Yah!" as he spurred it towards town, leaving a cloud of dust in his wake.

* * *

"Thank you, Sheriff. Thank you," Lionel blubbered as Mark turned the key in iron cell door and set him free.

"Don't thank me too much," Mark warned Lionel, "you ain't going anywhere yet." Nathan sat on the edge of Mark's desk, cradling a shotgun in his lap. Vincent stood by the jail's main door, his Winchester still clutched in his hands. Mark sat Lionel eying his deputies' weapons.

"Them guns ain't gonna do you no good," Lionel told them. "Those things are like something straight out of a nightmare."

"Ain't nothing on this Earth breathing that can't be killed," Vincent said. "You shoot anything enough, it's going to keel over eventually."

"I need to know everything you saw again." Mark plopped a chair in front of Lionel. "Might as well take a seat. I reckon this could take a while."

"I done told you everything, Sheriff," Lionel complained. "Weren't you listening? They're coming here. Maybe tonight, maybe tomorrow, but they're coming. If you're smart you'll clear out before they get here."

"Man's got a point," Nathan commented.

"This is my town," Mark snapped. "I ain't running from anything now or ever. Besides, all those folks in the street out there, they're depending on us to keep the peace. We were sworn in gentlemen and we have a duty to keep the peace even if it costs us our lives. You understand?"

"Yes, sir," Nathan answered weakly.

Mark whirled on Lionel. "Take a seat and start talking!"

Lionel sat down. "What do you want to know?"

Mark picked the stage driver's brain about the monsters: What they looked like, how fast they were, how strong. When Mark was done, the jail was silent.

"We need to send for help," Vincent added.

"It's too late," Mark said, shaking his head. "No one we sent would be able to get help and get back in time. Ain't got no choice but to deal with these things ourselves. Vincent, I want you to round up and deputize as many men as you can without causing a panic. Nathan, those railroad folk setting up a camp over at Sunrise Ridge, they got some dynamite. Get it and bring it here."

"Dynamite?" Nathan repeated.

"They can show you how to move it safely," Mark explained.

"What about you?" Vincent asked.

"You know I got to see to Marlene. If I don't, I won't be of any use to anyone."

As the sun set over the town of Seger, Mark began to regret his decision not to go public with what he knew. Even with the extra dozen men Vincent drafted to help, there was no hope of them protecting everyone. Mark opted to make their stand on Main Street. Regardless of which direction the monster came from, they'd end up on it eventually and they would be ready for it. Aside from the deputized men, Hank and Marlene were the only people to hear the truth of what was going on. Hank, of course, didn't believe any of it, or so he claimed, but Mark could see a light burning in the general store's window as he watched the street outside of the jail. Marlene sat on the edge of the cot in the cell closest to where he waited. A Colt lay on it beside her. She refused to even touch it but Mark had tried to show her how to use it if things fell apart. It was like pulling teeth to get her to go into the cell but Mark was betting that if he failed to stop the monsters, she'd slam the cell door fast enough for protection when the monsters came snarling into the jail. Those iron bars might just keep her alive. Nathan was on the roof of Hank's store with the dynamite and Vincent waited on the saloon's, acting as a lookout and providing cover fire for the men Mark had positioned in the street. The twelve new deputies were spread all over town, keeping to the shadows, guns ready, waiting on Hell to break loose. Mark had forbid Vincent from telling them what they were really up against. They believed a rogue band of Indians was coming to burn the town to the ground, but that didn't matter. They were all experienced and capable men, handpicked by Vincent. Mark had faith they would stand their ground and fight no matter what came at them.

Monster men, Mark bit his lip in thought. It didn't seem real despite the evidence to support Lionel's claim. But this was his town and he wasn't taking any chances. Mark had watched Lionel spend the only money he had to buy a horse and take off as he and his men made their preparations. Mark couldn't quite figure out if the stage driver was wiser than he was or just yellow. Wolves howled in the distance, then the screaming started.

Neil stood outside the barbershop with Ryan. Neil held a Winchester, fully loaded and ready. There was a chill in the night air. He tugged at his coat, pulling it tighter around his chest. If it weren't for his family, he would have never agreed to any of this when Vincent came calling. His fighting days were done long ago. He was pushing fifty and his hands weren't as fast as they used to be. "You should have brought a rifle," he told Ryan, watching the kid shove shells into his double barrel.

Ryan was a rough sort with a chip on his shoulder and known around town for his temper. He snorted at Neil, spitting into the dirt. "Mind your business, Pops. This here's got more stopping power and I don't own a rifle anyways."

"It's got a lot less range too," Neil commented. "You're gonna die trying to reload that thing, ya know?"

"You'll think different when the shooting starts and I'm the only thing keeping you alive as you're running for cover," Ryan boasted.

Neil remembered how much he was like Ryan when he was young and tried to hold his tongue. The kid was likely scared out of his mind and compensating with false bravado.

Ryan walked towards the side of the barbershop, heading for the alley beside it.

"Where you going?" Neil asked.

"Nature calls. What? You wanna come watch?"

Neil was about to stop him, tell him they should stick together, when a massive, hairy hand came out of the shadows, grabbing Ryan in a death grip. It yanked the young man out of sight behind the building. Ryan's shotgun went off, both barrels emptying with a flash to shatter the window of a shop across the street. Neil raised his Winchester to his shoulder, taking aim at the darkness beyond the corner of the barbershop. No sense in rushing to die. Give it time and death would come to him, and in doing so, it would expose itself.

Now Neil heard other guns firing around the town and men screaming their final words. He held his aim and waited. In seconds it emerged from an alley by the shop. A giant monster walking on two legs and standing, impossibly, nearly nine feet tall, Its eyes burned yellow and Ryan's blood dripped from the long claws on its hands and glistened in the hair around it mouth. Its arms were maliciously long and its back slightly hunched as it sniffed the air like a dog. It moved down the street slowly, looking for more prey, not seeming to notice him where he stood like a statue under the barbershop's awning. The red and blue swirled pole to his side was a grim warning that he may well end up in his own bloody bandages if he didn't get this next shot right. Neil squeezed the trigger of his rifle. His bullet caught the thing in the side of its skull. It grunted, staggering sideways as Neil let loose with more. He fired round after round, working his Winchester's lever. Blood splattered the wall of the tailor's shop behind the beast. The thing seemed to shake off the pain. It righted itself and charged at him. If his bullets were having any real effect, Neil couldn't see it.

As the creature drew closer, Neil flipped his rifle around in his hands to use it as a club. He swung its butt upwards in a wicked arc to connect with the underside of the monster's chin. Caught off balance by its adversary's desperate move, its head snapped back at an angle as it toppled sideways, crashing through the barbershop's window. Neil chucked his rifle, drawing his Colt as he made a run for it. With an angry roar, the creature flung itself into the street, chasing after him on all fours.

Neil's breath came in ragged gasps and his chest felt tight as he pushed on, running faster. The creature leapt at him, covering the distance between them. They both went rolling. It landed on top of him, pinning him down under its weight. Neil stuck his pistol into its gut, firing three times, point blank. The wolf monster whined. Neil tried to shove it off of him but it was just too strong. Its yellow eyes met his and Neil's bladder emptied itself. Warm liquid pooled underneath their struggling bodies. Then the unexpected happened. Neil heard the wolf laugh as a clawed hand tore into his forehead and the world went black.

* * *

Gerald was the sort of fellow who knew when to cut his losses and run and he was running now for his very life. The two monsters had come climbing down the side of the bank right on top of them. He'd seen the things rip Shane's warm, red, and purple guts from his stomach and toss Shane aside like a child's toy. Shane was a big man too. The kind no one in their right mind wanted to pick a fight with. Gerald had once seen Shane take on a whole gang of Mexicans in a bar fight and walk out with nothing more than a broken nose. He'd left two of the Mexicans dead and the others wishing they were. If these things could get him as easily as they had, Gerald sure wasn't so stupid as to try to fight them. He spurred the horse he'd stolen from outside the saloon, yelling and cursing for it to go faster. Its owner wasn't going to care he took it because Gerald figured whoever it was would be dead soon if they weren't already. The whole town would be dead if Shane was any indication. The monsters were giant wolves, . They came bounding after him as he kicked his horse harder still but it was like the animal was treading on molasses compared to the speed of the monsters. They overtook him before he was halfway to the edge of town. As the quicker of the two monsters reached for him, it stood up, running on two legs. One of its knife-like hands jerked Gerald from his saddle. He went flying into the other monster's path. Gerald screamed, trying to draw his Colt as the beast barreled into him. It swatted his pistol away, roaring, showing him a mouthful of red glistening, razor teeth. "Please!" Gerald shrieked as it leaned its head closer to his own and he smelt the beast's rancid breath. The monster plunged its hand into Gerald's chest and tore his heart through his rib cage. His eyes went wide as he slumped over, watching the monster take a bite from his still beating heart as he died.

* * *

Vincent was overwhelmed by the amount of targets he had to choose from. Neither he nor Mark imagined there would be so many of the monsters. The wolves were everywhere. He saw one of the things chasing a whore out of the saloon into the street below him and decided it was as good a target as any. He took aim and put a bullet into its spine. The wolf fell, twisting about in the dirt. *That'll teach you,* Vincent applauded himself. His victory was short lived. The wolf hopped up, its yellow eyes turning upwards to stare at his position. "Oh crap!" he cursed, levering another round into his Winchester's chamber. The monster moved in a blur. He barely had time to fire before it was leaping up onto the roof with him. His bullet sprayed blood as it hit the wolf-thing in its shoulder. Vincent backpedaled as it landed where he had been standing only a moment before.. Vincent's Winchester thundered as he emptied it into the monster's wide chest.

"Die you son of a . . . Die!" Vincent shouted.

Each round ripped away chunks of hair and flesh as they tore into the monster. It snarled at Vincent and reached out to grab him. Vincent ducked under the thing's arm, lunging to get away from it. Vincent's feet slipped on the spent casings from his rifle and he plummeted, careening off the roof. He landed on the street below with a dull thud. Vincent felt like his whole body was broken as he fought to stay conscious and roll over. Something heavy dropped onto his back. Fresh pain shot through him and blood erupted from his mouth like vomit as his internal organs were crushed into pulp.

* * *

Nathan watched it all from the roof of Hank's general store. He clutched a bundle of dynamite in his right hand and a match in his left but was too scared to use them. He told himself that if he just kept quiet and still the wolf-things would never notice him up here. There was a scuffle inside the store below and he knew the things were after Hank. He said a prayer for the grumpy old man but made no move to try to help him. A low, guttural growl came from somewhere behind where he knelt. Nathan turned slowly to look into the yellow eyes of one of the monsters. Out of instinct more than anything else, he stuck the match, lighting the dynamite's fuse. The wolf-thing stared, continuing to growl, but made no move to attack.

"I don't know what in the devil you are," Nathan said, finding his courage in the face of death, "but I reckon this here will kill even you."

The wolf-thing tilted its head as it understood the words. Then the crackling sparks raced along the bundle of dynamite's short fuse reached the explosives.

* * *

"Get down!" Mark screamed inside the jail as the explosion shook the town. He hit the floor just as the jail's window blew inward. Shards of broken glass rained over him. In the wake of the explosion, the town of Seger was quiet once more. Mark hauled himself up from the floor to peek out the jail's smashed window to the street outside. Over a dozen of the wolf-things stared back at him. Some sat on their haunches, others stood on two legs like men.

"That was a good try, Sheriff," one of the things growled. "Best I've seen yet, to be honest." The wolf-thing sniffed the air. "Do I smell a woman in there? How kind of you to rustle us up some fun. With the killing done, the boys sure could use some release to wind down with."

Mark jerked up his rifle and put a bullet into the talking wolf's mouth. Brain matter splattered from the backside of its skull as the bullet exited its body. It spun about in place and dropped to the ground as a chorus of howls and snarls rose in the night. The wolves rushed forward.

* * *

Samuel looked down into the town of Seger from the hill above it. Fires raged where its general store had once stood. He smiled contently knowing the first part of his work here was finished. Seger was his to do with as he wished. The town was as good a place as any to make a temporary home and wait for his family to catch up with him. Besides, the few survivors his men would have left alive to be converted would require a couple of days to adjust to their new life before they would make good soldiers in his ever-growing army. Samuel felt the night shift around him like reality itself was bending and he knew his partner had arrived. He turned as an effeminate man in his late twenties, with well cut blonde hair under a bowler cap, emerged from the bushes. The man was dressed in white from head to toe. He wore no gun belt nor appeared to carry any kind of weapon.

"You're late," Samuel announced.

The man cocked his head, popping the joints of his neck loudly as he did so. "Ran into a bunch of Calvary chaps in California. Didn't want to leave them without a proper goodbye."

"Everything is progressing according to plan," Samuel told him proudly.

"Your plan. How are you holding up? Is the spirit giving you problems?"

Samuel laughed. "Do you take me for a novice? I hunger more but not so much as to let it interfere with my work."

"Good." The man in white removed his pearl-colored gloves. "It's nice to have someone who shares my vision for a change, even it is a rather distorted view."

Samuel's gaze returned to the town of Seger. "With the new recruits converted here we should have the strength to move on Washington after we bring Texas to its knees."

"Your control over them is strong," the man in white commented, as if he could personally feel the bond between Samuel and his soldiers.

"As it should be," Samuel agreed.

"And my payment?"

"My brother Shannon is in Texas. I didn't believe he would join the others to come after me but you were right about that as well." Samuel tried not to sound too impressed. "Why him? What's so special about Shannon?"

"A wolf who wants to be human?" the man in white giggled. "He is a rare and beautiful thing not to be wasted. The angels in Heaven will cry when he falls. I do so love the rain, don't you?"

Samuel grunted. "You immortals and your games. What do they gain you in the end?"

The man in white said nothing for a moment. He only smiled. "Some of your children are on their way, to boast of their victory no doubt."

Samuel glared at the man in white. "Our agreement forbids you from harming them," Samuel reminded him.

"So it does. Nonetheless, I believe I shall stick around for a while. If the saloon is still standing I could use a drink."

Two wolves came bounding onto the hilltop with them. Their flesh melted, their bodies twisting and reshaping as they became men. Ed and Kevin were both taken aback by the man in white. Samuel could see the man's scent frightened them. "Allow me to introduce our ally," Samuel said quickly before they tried something foolish.

"Pleased to meet you," the man in white said, bowing to them as he rolled his cap down the length of his arm to catch it in his hand, allowing his flaxen hair to catch the moonlight. "It's really such a pleasure to meet you boys."

Always with the showmanship, Samuel thought, disgusted, but he managed to hold his tongue. *At least the man in white didn't speak in rhymes.*

"We kept the sheriff alive for you," Ed told him, like a kid expecting a reward for thinking ahead. "Figured you might want a meal too, boss."

"You boys go ahead," the man in white ordered. "I'll catch up shortly."

If the man in white possessed the power to match their speed as wolves, he wasn't ready or willing to reveal it. Samuel nodded at him and dropped to the ground, shifting fully into a wolf before his hands, now paws, touched the earth. Ed and Kevin followed his example, chasing after him, as they raced on four legs towards Seger.

* * *

Tears ran down Mark's cheeks, leaving trails in the blood and dirt covering them. The pain was close to being unbearable. The wolves had sliced his Achilles' tendons and bound his hands together with a heavy chain, suspending him from it on a spike driven into the saloon's wall just outside the building's entrance. The chains cut into the flesh of his wrists from the weight of his body. For some reason beyond his understanding, the wolves had kept a couple dozen of the town's residents alive, albeit beaten into unconsciousness. The others were all dead, now just meat filling their bellies. Marlene suffered neither of those fates. The beasts had torn through the iron bars protecting her and dragged her into the street outside the jail. Their claws shredded her clothing until she was so close to naked as not to matter. The wolf Mark had shot in the mouth held his head and forced him to watch as the others in his pack took turns with her, in every hole, as she cried his name over and over begging for help. When she finally bled out, the wolves kept at her until well after her corpse had grown cold.

The wolves or demons or whatever they were wore the forms of men now, having transformed before his eyes. They partied, got drunk, and fired their guns into the night sky like any victorious army would. There were too many of them for Mark to keep track of as they came and went from the saloon. Many of them would poke at him or whisper some kind of cruel insult into his ear as they pricked his flesh with their overly long fingernails. A small group of them waited outside the saloon like dogs waiting for their master to return. Three wolves appeared on the edge of town, running towards them. They too became men. The ones who had been waiting offered them clothing. One of these new arrivals stood out among the others as they got dressed. His silver eyes lit up the darkness. He donned a thick, black robe instead of proper clothing and strolled leisurely over to stare at Mark. His appraising look sent a shiver through Mark as he spoke.

"Good evening, Sheriff. I'm told you put up quite a fight for one of your kind. The boys tell me one of your men even managed to kill one of us by setting off some kind of explosion on top of the general store."

"So you can die," Mark tried to laugh but it came out as a cough that shook his body, causing the chains holding him to cut even deeper into the skin of his wrists. Mark gritted his teeth and met the man's silver eyes. "That's good to know because if you let me loose, I will send you to Hell."

"Who said anything about letting you live?" the wolfman chuckled. Another man, dressed entirely in white, stepped from the shadows behind his tormentor. Mark wondered how he hadn't noticed the man before. The man's spotless attire gleamed like an angel's aura as he moved closer to Mark. The man in white leaned in, saying his name like they were old friends, "Mark, Hell isn't such a bad place. Trust me, I should know." He grabbed Mark's groin, crushing his privates into nothing more than a red smear. Mark distantly heard the echoes of his own voice wailing through the streets of Seger.

* * *

Higgins and Father Jericho kept their heads low. The odds of even one of the werewolves seeing them this far away were next to nil but it was better not to take chances. They shared Higgins' looking glass, taking turns with it.

"We're too late," Higgins told the priest.

"Or perhaps, we've come just in time. The Lord moves in mysterious ways."

"All those people dead. Why are they doing this, Father? If these creatures have always existed, like you say, why haven't they done this before?"

"One question at a time." Father Jericho's Bible was fastened to his belt next to his silver tomahawk as if it too were a weapon. "Regardless, I don't know the answer to your first inquiry but as to your second, I believe there are more forces at work here then we're aware of. Let me ask you, Colonel, have you ever heard the tales of a strange man who wears only white and has a voice like the choirs of Heaven?"

"Can't say as I have," Higgins admitted, not having a clue where the priest was headed with this line of talk.

"Some say he's an angel descended to this Earth but he's not. I've spent the last five years of my life searching for him. I've seen his works and they are not of God."

"I ain't following you, Father."

"The stories of him predate the colonies founded when this great nation was born. The Indians call him *the soulless one who rides with death*."

Father Jericho handed Higgins back his looking glass. "Look carefully at the figures in front of the saloon. That's him, Colonel."

"He's not one of the wolves?"

"No, he's much more and worse than that."

Higgins was growing frustrated. "Father, we don't have time for games and vague answers."

"He is Legion," Father Jericho said with an odd mix of fear and respect.

"This doesn't change anything, Father. Whoever. . . Whatever his is, we're still going down there and killing every blasted one of those abominations."

"Do you have a plan on how to do that, Colonel? If so, I would be keen to hear it. We're outgunned and outnumbered."

"I have lived through rougher spots than this," Higgins boasted.

"Against men, perhaps, Colonel. Tell me, do you even have enough silver to kill them all?"

"You told me fire killed them too."

"It does."

"Then you let me worry about the wolves and you handle that feller you're so scared of."

"Agreed," Father Jericho nodded.

"Come on," Higgins said, "we need to get back to the men."

* * *

"Listen," Sarah said, bringing her horse to a stop on the outskirts of the town ahead of them, hushing her brothers' conversation. "You smell that?"

Shannon and Graham rode up beside her. Shannon sniffed the air. "What is that?"

Graham touched the brim of his hat, pulling it lower to block the light of the rising sun. "You've been out of the game too long." Graham drew his revolver, checking its cylinder to make sure it was fully loaded.

"Graham, are those silver bullets?" Sarah asked.

Shannon could see the way the rays of the sun reflected off the bullets in the gun and knew that they were.

Graham didn't answer. He flipped his pistol closed. "Best get this over with."

"Wait a minute," Shannon told him, "You think Graham is here?"

"The air stinks of things that would be wolves," Sarah growled. "Not like us, Shannon."

"Surely Samuel wouldn't. . ."

"He's insane, Shannon," Graham cut him off. "I told you that."

"What's the hold up?" Zed asked, "We doing this or not."

Shannon saw the violence waiting to be let loose in Zed's posture. Yule was snarling, his teeth no longer those of a man's, at the scent of the Changed. Shannon hadn't encountered one of the Changed in decades. They weren't anything like the family. The Changed had no laws to govern them, no tradition to cling to and give them purpose. Most of them didn't even truly understand what they were. The Changed were the victims of pure bloods like the family who had been bitten or scratched but somehow survived the encounter. Usually a pure blood made sure their prey was dead but no one was perfect. These poor souls found their lives forever changed with the next full moon. Few of the Changed stayed sane after their first transformation. Fewer still overcame the new primal urges that drove them. Pure bloods killed the Changed on sight. The feral monsters had no place in this world. They were the basis of the legends the humans believed in and the reason Shannon's kind was feared. Not that the pure bloods themselves didn't give the humans reasons enough for that themselves. To knowingly change someone was a crime that could not be forgiven. If Samuel had crossed that line, there was no hope for him.

"Shannon," Zed said, "what did I tell you about thinking too much?"

With a battle cry, Zed kicked his horse, charging into the town.

"Dang it, Zed!" Sarah swore.

As the family reached the town of Franklin's main street, Zed was already there and waiting for them. Zed whistled loudly. "Somebody's really tore up this place," he said.

"Where is everyone?" Yule asked.

"Dead. Dead or changed and moved on," Graham explained.

The giant's face was full of disappointment.

"For Heaven's sake, Graham," Sarah said, "how crazy is Samuel? Think about the amount of attention a massacre like this is going to attract."

Shannon frowned. "You know what he's planning, don't you?"

Graham stayed silent.

"Graham," Zed warned him.

"I might know a little more than I let on," Graham admitted. Shannon knew Graham hadn't told the others that Samuel had found what he been seeking all these years. "Samuel found the Wendigo," he heard himself say aloud.

Zed's mouth dropped open, Sarah snarled, and Yule reached over, plucking Graham from his horse's saddle. As Graham dangled, his feet kicking above the street, Yule roared, "Graham!"

"Put him down, Yule," Sarah cautioned the giant. Shannon saw her hand disappear underneath the folds of her duster. Yule flung Graham into the dirt. Graham bounced twice from the force of Yule's throw before he came to rest, lying on his side.

"It's not Graham's fault," Shannon said. "We're all to blame. None of us believed it was real. Still not sure I do. But all of us knew Samuel wanted its power from the time he was able to read."

Zed dismounted, helping Graham to his feet. "Give me one of those cigars of yours," Zed ordered him, "I need a bloody smoke."

Zed lit up, puffing on it furiously. "This kind of changes things, don't it? It ain't about blood anymore. This here's pure old good versus evil."

"Are we the good guys?" Yule asked.

"Oh God help us," Sarah muttered.

"We all knew Samuel was dangerous," Shannon looked at the others. "What else do you know, Graham?"

"I told you, he's building an army."

"An army of the Changed," Sarah pointed out.

Graham nodded. "I don't know how, maybe it's the power of the Wendigo, but he's controlling them. Once he's ready, he'll move on Washington DC and bring the United States to its knees."

"You think he's after political power too?" Sarah asked.

"No, Washington is a symbol of freedom and what mankind can achieve. Samuel wants to see it burn and send a message to the world that humanity's time is over. He won't stop there. He'll keep going until the whole of the world is either changed or dead."

"If the Wendigo is inside him, just how in Hell are we supposed to stop him, Graham?" Zed flicked what was left of his cigar away. "Ain't none of us that know anything about all that magic crap."

"We'll find a way," Shannon spoke up before Graham could answer. "We don't have any choice."

Always the tactician, Sarah turned to him. "And the Changed? How many does he have by now? A couple dozen? Hundreds? What do we do about them? They're weaker but there's only five of us, Shannon. Five." She raised a hand, showing him the number with her lean fingers.

"One good thing," Zed commented, "they'll be easy to track. Those Changed buggers stink like a field full of horse manure. They're headed south."

"We're gonna need some more silver," Sarah said. "Any ideas where we're gonna get it?"

Graham smiled. "That part I got covered."

* * *

The wolves were overconfident. That was something Higgins could use and he did. The few men they posted as lookouts were a joke. Whoever was leading the creatures had no understanding of military tactics. The wolves left themselves wide open to attack. Higgins, knowing he was outgunned, decided to split his force into three units. The two smaller ones would hit the town from the east and west sides, drawing fire and creating a diversion for his main battle group to ride in, guns blazing right into the middle of Seger. He hoped most of the wolves would be dead before they realized what was happening. The only real problem with his plans was that his supply of silver was limited. Divided up, each of his soldiers carried only three rounds that were going to matter. He'd instructed them all to make sure those shots counted. They had to attack before nightfall. The wolves' advantage would be too great in the darkness. Father Jericho had left them to pray in solitude as they made their preparations for the attack. Higgins hoped the Lord would hear the crazy priest's prayers. They would need all the help they could get.

The priest had given him a silver dagger. Higgins rolled it over in his hands, examining the blade. It was well balanced and sharper than it appeared. If the wolves got close enough for him to have to use it . . . Well, Higgins didn't want to dwell on that possibility too much. He had one more surprise for the wolves. In addition to their normal weapons, three men in each of the smaller units, as well as everyone in the main group, carried a bottle of highly flammable lamp oil they'd looted from Franklin. He imagined the wolves' howls as they burned. The images made him smile.

Two hours before sunset, the men were ready. Father Jericho joined Higgins as he gave the signal to set things into motion.

* * *

Corporal Trantham was in charge of the dozen men moving in from the East. Seger was a big town. This side of it was buffered by a railroad station. Trantham and his men crept over the tracks on foot. They were to the station and peering down one of the town's streets before they saw their first set of wolves. They came stepping out of what appeared to be a general store. Only one of them wore a holstered gun on his hip. Trantham figured if you could turn into a giant monster, guns weren't something you worried too much about.

His men spread out to both sides of the street, taking cover in doorways and behind an overturned wagon someone must have tried to use to as an escape vehicle when the wolves had come. Trantham knew when the shooting started things were going to get ugly fast, but that was the job. You either got used to it or you got dead. Shouldering his Winchester, he took aim at the burly wolf on the right. It had a cigarette in its lips and a bottle of whiskey in its hands. Trantham steadied himself, took a breath, and pulled the trigger. The rifle bucked in his hands as the wolf's forehead exploded into a mass of pulped red meat. Its body crumpled over as the other wolf opened his mouth to scream or howl. Trantham never found out which the wolf intended to do. One of his men dropped it with a shot that sent the wolf spinning and careening through the general store's window with a sibilant crash. Trantham could hear voices yelling and shooting in the distance. Some of those voices changed into howls. Trantham worked his Winchester's lever, chambering another round. Two more shots, he thought, hoping he lived to see the sun go down. A pack of wolves rounded the corner of the street and came towards their position. These creatures were fully transformed into massive real wolves and dang, they were fast. Trantham's next shot missed, sending up a puff of dust in the street where it struck just beyond a sprinting wolf. He cursed, deciding it was time to play dirty. "Toss 'em!"

Two of his men lit up bottles of oil and threw them at the wolves. An explosion of fire filled the street in front of the group's position, catching on the animal's wiry hair. Of the eight wolves, only two escaped the flames unscathed. They came bounding onward. One took a round to its side that sprayed blood. The wolf yelped, its pace slowing. Two more bullets ripped into its flesh, sending it on to Hell.

"Watch the ammo!" Trantham shouted. None of them could afford to waste bullets. The remaining wolf leapt, taking one of his men to the ground as it landed. It tore out the private's throat before a bullet slammed into the backside of its head. A Winchester fired five times somewhere behind Trantham's position. "Dang it!" Trantham screamed, getting ready to kill whoever was firing so many rounds as the soldier beside him took a round to his chest. He died as it entered his heart, grasping at Trantham's uniform as his corpse fell at the Corporal's feet. A wolf, still half in human form, was running towards them from the rear. The wolfman loosed a second series of shots as Trantham dove for cover in the general store's doorway.

That's just not fair, Trantham thought as two more of his men died. He peeked around the doorway and fired off his last silver bullet. It caught the wolfman in his shoulder, causing him to lose his grip on his Winchester. The man's skin was sprouting thick, black hair and his neck was elongating as he disappeared into the rail station's ticket booth. Trantham didn't know if the silver would act like poison in the creature's blood stream and kill the man or if he was merely wounded. He didn't have time to worry about it either. Several of the burning wolves had recovered from the initial shock and pain from the flames raging over their bodies. A chorus of quick, well placed shots from his men finished the creatures. Trantham could hear gunfire and screams everywhere. A low growl came from close above him. He looked up to see one of the wolves in its monster form as it sprang from the building's roof at him. Its claws took his eyes, mangling the flesh of his face in a single vicious swipe.

* * *

Higgins led the charge into town, his horse's feet kicking up dirt from its speed. The thirty odd men of the main battle group followed after him. Heavy black smoke rose above the town of Seger on both its east and west sides. He'd ordered every single soldier in his group not to open fire until they were on the town's main street.

As they entered Seger, the wolves were ready for them. *Someone new must be directing them,* Higgins thought, cursing under his breath. Numerous wolves in half-humanoid form accompanied by dozens more on four legs sprinted towards Higgins and his men. Several horses panicked. Their riders died under the hooves of those behind them. Higgins kept his steed under control as he scrutinized the wolves in human form lining the roofs for the buildings on both sides of Seger's main street. He ducked, riding low. The next thing he knew, his horse was rearing up as a monster wolf met it head on. He heard the horse's ribs folding inward from the impact as he was flung from his saddle. He hit the ground, rolling. A four-legged wolf pounced onto his chest, pinning him down. He yanked the dagger Father Jericho had given him from the sheath on the side of his boot, plunging it into the wolf's stomach. The wolf shrieked as he twisted the blade deeper. With a grunt he shoved the dead wolf aside and scurried to his feet. Higgins drew his pistol as four more wolves came snarling at him. He spotted the saloon and darted for its batwing doors. The corpse of a man who appeared to have been tortured, with a Rorschach blood stain on the groin of his pants, hung nailed to the building's wall beside the doorway.

Higgins threw himself inside. The doors flopped inward as the wolves bumped them with the tops of their heads as they entered. Higgins lay on the dirty, wooden floor. He raised his pistol at the wolves and put a round into the nearest one as it jumped at him. It died before it thudded to the floor in front of him. He waited for death, knowing the other wolves would be on him before he could get off another shot but it didn't come.

The remaining three wolves had turned to face the door. Father Jericho stood there. A pistol in one hand, his tomahawk in the other. The wolves appeared confused, not quite sure what to make of the crazy priest. Father Jericho whipped up his pistol. Two of the wolves were dead before they could move. The third charged him. Father Jericho's tomahawk met its skull, splitting it open to reveal the gray brain matter inside it. Father Jericho put a boot on the wolf's corpse and jerked his tomahawk free. Outside the saloon, the sound of gunfire was sparser and more erratic. Higgins started for the door. Jericho blocked his path.

"You can't help them. Your men are dead."

Higgins moved to toss the priest out of his way but a voice as sweet as honeysuckle stopped him. It came from the saloon's upper floor. "Colonel Higgins," it called, "how good of you to join us!"

The voice belonged to a man dressed entirely in white who swaggered down the stairs to greet them. The man's gaze fell upon Father Jericho. "And you brought a priest with you. How quaint."

As the man in white reached the bottom of the stars, another man in black robes, with eyes as silver as Seated Liberty dollars, emerged from the rear of the saloon.

"Allow me to introduce my associate, Samuel." The man in white clicked his tongue, raising a hand to his ear as he made show of listening to the dying sound of battle outside. "I fear your men aren't faring very, well, Colonel. Maybe next time, you should bring more silver bullets if you're planning to attack an entire town full of werewolves."

Samuel growled at the man in white. "Kill them and be done with it."

The man in white laughed. "My friend Samuel isn't quite as civilized as I am, Colonel. I think a man should know the one who takes his life so he can remember them as he's burning in the fires of Hell."

"Am I supposed to guess who you are?" Higgins asked. "You haven't told me your name."

"Names are so unimportant, don't you think? I have had so many, I can't honestly recall them all."

"You are Lucifer," Father Jericho shouted, taking aim at the man in white with his pistol. "And by the power of the all mighty God, I command you to depart."

The man in white was on Father Jericho before Higgins could so much as blink. He swatted Father Jericho's gun from his hand and lifted him off the floor with a single hand about the priest's neck. Father

Jericho tried to bring his tomahawk into play but it burst into flames, the metal bubbling away into nothingness from the heat. The priest struggled against the man in white's hold, his face turning blue from the death grip cutting off his ability to breath.

"Father," the man in white said, "Your faith is tainted and weak."

Higgins heard a snapping sound as the priest's head jerked to one side. The man in white cast Father Jericho's corpse aside like rubbish. Samuel advanced on him as Higgins took a step back. Blue energy, like lightning, crackled and danced over the wolfman's fingers.

"No," the man in white ordered Samuel. Samuel snarled back but stopped where he was.

"My dear Colonel Higgins, we could use a man such as yourself." The man in white shook his head sadly."For all his power and knowledge, my friend Samuel just doesn't have a military mind like you. Join him and lead his army and you can know a life that will span centuries. His kind doesn't age like normal men."

"And if I refuse?" Higgins asked.

The man in white waved a hand at Father Jericho's corpse. Maggots erupted from the priest's skin, burrowing through it to eat away at his flesh. Legions of the tiny, white, disgusting things swarmed the priest's body, squirming rapidly like sand grains in a tornado. In seconds, all that remained were the priest's bones. Higgins fell to his knees, vomiting up his last meal.

"Well then," the man in white giggled, "you could be like him."

The man in white moved to stand over him as his body still shook with dry heaves.

"Shall I take that as a yes, then?"

Higgins looked up into the angelic features of the man in ashen face, so perfect and girlishly handsome.

"Yes," he said weakly, wiping at his mouth.

The man in white waved Samuel forward. "Change him then."

* * *

The family abandoned their horses. They could move faster as wolves. Only Yule kept a two-legged form, carrying their clothes and weapons in a massive pack tied to his shoulders. Shannon and the rest of the family left him behind as they darted across the last stretch of land between them and the train they planned to intercept. Graham's contacts in the government had given him its location and route. It was carrying a shipment of silver headed northwards to a storage facility where it would be kept until it could be melted down into real currency. Their plan was to rob the train and take the silver they needed to stop Samuel's army of the Changed. Normal train robbers might have stooped to blocking the tracks or destroying them to force the train into braking but the family had no need of such tactics.

The train pulled six cars behind its engine. Two of them were open boxcars containing armed soldiers. The other cars were enclosed, containing weapons, horses, and the silver. The family split up as they neared the tracks. The soldiers aboard the open cars were pointing at them. Certainly no normal wolves would behave as they were. One of the men in the forward car started taking pop shots at them as his companions cheered him on. Shannon stood out among the family, his hair stark white like an arctic wolf. He zigged and zagged, dodging the man's poorly aimed shots with ease. Zed veered away from the rest of the family as Graham, Sarah, and Shannon headed straight on towards the train. Soon several other soldiers joined the hunt, their Winchesters cracking. Puffs of dirt and small rocks jumped into the air as their rounds pelted the ground all around the charging family. The conductor must have thought they were under attack because the train began to accelerate.

Shannon saw Graham take a bullet in one of his legs and falter, losing speed. The soldiers were all screaming as Shannon and Sarah reached the train, shifting into monster form, leaping onto the train. Sarah took the forward car, Shannon the rear one. Shannon flung men from the train, trying to kill as few as possible. Sarah wasn't so kind. As she landed amid the soldiers of the forward car, three of them fired point blank into her chest and stomach. She staggered but still recovered too fast for the men to take advantage of her pain. The claws of her right hand sank into one soldier's stomach, emerging through his back. Blood flew over her hair as she yanked her hand upwards, tearing the man in half. Her left hand backhanded another soldier, breaking his neck upon impact and flinging him into the ranks of his panicked friends. Bullets whizzed by her but she crouched and several of the fear-crazed soldiers shot each other. As she leapt up, her teeth closed on one of the men's throat. She ripped away a chunk in an explosion of red wetness. A brave soldier pressed the barrel of his Colt into the hair on the back of her head. She started to snarl and whirl about to yank his arm from his body but the soldier managed to pull the trigger. The bullet caught her in her left eye, reducing it to pulp. Sarah felt it plunging into the gray matter of her brain before it fragmented the bones of her skull and left a gaping hole behind her left ear. Sarah slumped to the car's floor. The six remaining soldiers towered over her unconscious form, emptying their rifles into her twitching body.

"Sarah!" Shannon screamed as he ran across the roofs of the other cars between them to come to her aid. The train's brakes squealed and the inertia sent the soldiers bouncing off the car's walls as Shannon leapt into it. Shannon's large, white-haired monster form loomed above them as he saw the fear in their eyes. His fist caved in one soldier's face like a melon. Hee crushed another's skull on the floor with his foot. A soldier drew his sidearm like a professional gunfighter, flipping its hammer with one hand while the other pulled its trigger. The bullets sinking into his flesh only made Shannon angrier. He grabbed the man by his jaw, jerking him off the floor to bite into the top of his head through his hat. Hot blood gushed over Shannon's tongue.

Zed appeared from the train's engine wearing the conductor's cap and nothing else, and leapt onto the edge of the car's front side. With a smile, he dropped the last of the soldiers in the car with Shannon, along with a Colt he must have taken from the soldier riding shotgun in the engine car. The sight of him standing there naked, hairless, with only the ostentatious hat and a smoking six-gun made Sarah laugh as her eye finished regenerating and she came to—much to Shannon's relief.

"That's just wrong," she commented "No offense, Zed, but couldn't you have kept your hair on?"

Zed cackled. "You know me, I like to make an entrance."

Yule came lumbering from the trees. He tossed Zed his clothes. "Get dressed!" the giant roared. "You're scaring me, brother."

Graham was with him, already dressed in his expensive, black suit and puffing on a cigar. "Yule, if you'll be so kind as to open the cars for us."

Yule grunted and moved to the cars, the muscles of his thick, hair-covered arms bulging as his claws sank into the wood of the doors. He yanked away each of the heavy doors, tossing them aside. Graham stood, almost drooling, as he stared at the silver they had come for. Zed however, tugging on his pants, hopped over to the car full of weapons and ammo. "Is that what I think it is?" he asked, eying a shining, band new Gatling gun.

Shannon, still in his monster form like Yule and Sarah, walked up to Zed and slapped him on the shoulder. "Looks like Christmas came early this year, huh?"

* * *

Higgins' mouth opened in a silent scream as the bones of his body broke and grew. His brown eyes blazed yellow as tears rolled down his cheeks and his face extended forward, becoming a snout. His teeth clattered to the saloon's wooden floor as longer, razored ones pushed through the flesh of his gums. When it was over, he stood nine feet tall, panting, and filled with a supernatural hunger for raw meat, human or otherwise. His head whipped around to stare at Samuel and the man in white.

"Down, boy," the man instructed him from the corner of the bar where he sat with a glass of congealing blood in his hand. Higgins bent his head back in a roar so loud it shook the bottles on the shelf behind the saloon's counter.

"What did you do?" Higgins heard Samuel asking as power flowed through his veins. He felt more alive than he ever had.

"I can't control him," Samuel admitted.

"I put a piece of me in his heart. Thought it would make things more interesting," the man in white giggled.

"But I thought you gave him to me, to be my general for the attack?"

"Step into the street and take a look at your army, Samuel. Good old Higgins here and his boys did some real damage to your little army. You'll need to hit another town on your way east to replace your losses. That's going to slow you down."

"So?" Samuel growled.

"So, I am getting tired of waiting on your family to show. Higgins here is going to bring your brother, Shannon, to me. I am done waiting."

Higgins nodded his massive, new head at his master's words.

"You know they're coming!" Samuel's voice rose in pitch. "How can you abandon us now when we're so close?"

"Oh please, Samuel. I know you'll be happy when I am gone. Don't pretend that you need me. I know how you like being top dog. Except for your payment, our bargain is finished." The man in white got to his feet.

"I will not allow this thing you've made," Samuel waved at Higgins, "to slay my family. They are mine and mine alone to do with as I see fit. Except for Shannon!"

The man in white shrugged. "Come on, Higgins, it's time to leave."

Higgins heard Samuel make a noise through his teeth like a low whistle too quiet for a human to hear. But before he could warn his master, the saloon's wall exploded inward as two huge werewolves entered. Another came smashing through the saloon's already partial-ly-shattered window to land on the other side of the man in white. Higgins waited for the command to shred them into strips of mangled meat with his claws but it never came. His master glanced at Samuel with a frown on his lips and said, "Really?"

"Your kind are known for their lies," Samuel roared. Then calming some, he said, "They are my family and I will be the one who sends them screaming to Hell. Not some foppish immortal who acts like a woman and his demon-wolf pet!"

The man in white moved so fast even Higgins' heightened senses and reflexes could barely keep up with him. His arms burst into masses of tentacles with spear-like tips, impaling the two wolves who'd entered through the wall. The tentacles writhed inside of them, tearing through the flesh of their bodies, and snaking back around to protrude from their chests, eyes, mouths, and the flesh of their arms. In an instant, the man in white's tentacles were regular arms again. A small, silver blade gleamed as it flew from his hand to embed itself between the eyes of the third wolf by the window. It toppled forward into the floor, instantly dead. Samuel shoved both of his hands forward at the man in white, screaming in some kind of ancient language Higgins' had never heard before. Blue lightning crackled at his master. The man in white raised a hand to block the bolts. They ricocheted away from him harmlessly, setting fire to the ceiling, the bar, and several parts of the saloon's floor as Higgins dodged, avoiding one that came in his direction.

"Samuel," the man in white warned, "I am willing to overlook this little outburst of yours given what you carry inside you but stop now."

Samuel lowered his hands, defeated. Higgins smelt fear coming from him in waves.

"Leave then!" Samuel raged.

Higgins watched the man in white tip his hat at Samuel as the saloon burned around them. "Nice doing business with you," the man in white smiled. "Come, Higgins, it's time for us to take our leave. We have wolves to hunt."

Samuel watched them vanish into the horizon as he stood in the saloon's doorway. Ed and Kevin stood with him.

"Boss?" Ed asked. "You want us to go after them?"

"No," Samuel answered, shaking his head, "we've got more important things to do."

Samuel walked into the street. The latest batch of converts awaited him there. They were all in wolf form. His magic had brought on their first transformation early, as he had no time to wait for a full moon. He looked into the dozen or so new snarling faces of his army and smiled. "Welcome," he told them, "welcome to the future! You are no longer mere, mortal humans! You are the beasts of the night who strike fear into the hearts of men, and soon this nation will tremble before our power!"

* * *

The family continued south on Samuel's trail. They'd claimed the horses on the train they'd robbed as their own to help carry their new gear and weapons. As always, Graham's pheromones calmed the beasts into submission to make them docile enough to ride. The family had taken a day to fashion the silver-coated bullets and weapons they would need to confront Samuel's army of the Changed. Only Zed's speed and skill allowed them to do it so quickly.

Yule carried the Gatling gun they'd found, remaining in monster form, in his saddle. Graham complained endlessly about it. He swore it made the horses far more difficult to control with such a blatant and instinctual threat riding among them. Zed was disappointed that Yule claimed the Gatling but in reality, Zed would never have been able to use it like Yule intended to and the added mobility of the weapon would give the family a huge advantage over Samuel's forces. They all could tell they were getting close. The scent of the Changed was so powerful, it meant either Samuel was within a matter of miles from where they were or his army was larger than they'd guessed.

Sarah rode next to Shannon. Her eyes were full of regret and sadness whereas Zed and Yule were practically bursting with anticipation for the battle to come. Even Graham seemed eager to have it over with. Shannon knew there was more to her emotions than the dark task ahead. Sarah was a warrior, more so than any of the rest of them.

"Want to talk about it?" Shannon asked.

"Those soldiers on the train. . . They got the drop on me," Sarah said.

"It happens."

"Not to me, it doesn't. You know that."

Shannon shrugged. "We all have bad days."

"I was watching you," Sarah admitted quietly. "I love you Shannon. I always have."

"You're my sister," he said simply, not wanting to go down the road they were heading for in this conversation.

"It's more than that whether you want to address it or not. You're a distraction. I can't focus with you around."

"So I should leave then?" Shannon asked, knowing he couldn't do any such thing until after they'd dealt with Samuel.

"When you left the pack, I was crushed, Shannon. It's why I left too. I traveled the world trying to get over you and move on."

"I thought you were searching for peace."

"Peace, sure. I wanted to make the pain go away. When we were growing up, you were always the good one. You tried so hard to be more than you were. I admired you so much. Before I knew it, my admiration and crush had become so much more. We're not humans, Shannon, not matter how much you want to be. My feelings aren't wrong."

"I'm sorry Sarah but to me it is. You're my sister," Shannon said gently.

"It's not your fault, Shannon, you can't control how I feel but it's not something I can just let go of either."

"And me being back is why you're so depressed now?" Shannon asked, hoping there was more to what was going on with her than just her feelings for him.

"You're certainly part of the problem," Sarah frowned, "but don't you feel it? Something's not right. It's like there's a scent underneath that of Samuel and his Changed, so faint and yet so strong at the same time. Whatever it is, it's old, Shannon. Older than our kind."

"I believe you." Shannon gave her a sympathetic look. "What do you think it is?"

"That's just it, Shannon. I don't know but it reeks of death and evil."

"Maybe it has something to do with Samuel's magic?"

Sarah shook her head as Graham slowed his horse, falling back from the lead and joining them. "Hate to interrupt but Yule and Zed are driving me crazy. I can't listen to them placing bets about who's going to rack more of a body count when we find Samuel's army of Changed."

"It's okay, Graham," Sarah told him, "We were done here anyway."

Shannon watched as she kicked her horse and galloped on ahead of them.

"Never seen her like that before," Graham commented. As Shannon watched him reach for a cigar from the case in his jacket, all Hell broke loose.

A monster the size of Yule came tearing out of the bushes alongside the trail they rode on. It yanked Zed from his saddle and hurled him over the cliff to their right. He fell screaming into the darkness below. Shannon saw the monster was like one of the Changed but not really one of them. There was something different about it. It went at Yule as the giant leapt from his saddle to meet it. The Gatling gun fell from his hands forgotten. Shannon watched and knew his brother was making a mistake.

"What in the Hades?" Graham shouted. The creature had achieved the impossible, slipping up on them all.

Yule delivered a blow that sent teeth flying from the monster's mouth as his massive fist connected with the thing's jaw. Its green eyes burnt like emeralds as it tore into Yule with a speed that matched Zed's, landing more punches than Shannon would've thought possible in such a small amount of time. Yule staggered under its fury. The creature closed in for the kill as Sarah jumped from her horse and ran at it. Three spinning, bladed stars coated in silver flew from her hand. The thing howled as the stars thunked into it. It whirled on Sarah, lashing out at her. Shannon saw her duck under its swing as she drew two silver daggers from underneath her duster. Launching herself at the thing, she screamed a battle cry, her eyes blazing yellow, as she drove both daggers to their hilts into the thing's chest. The creature stared down at her, unfazed, as Sarah looked up at it. It grabbed her by the hair, knocking off her hat.

"Hey!" Shannon yelled at it. It threw Sarah from its path. She squealed as half of her hair stayed in its hand. She went flying to roll along the side of the trail. The creature came at him and Graham. Both of them were still in their saddles with their Colts drawn. They emptied their pistols into the creature in a blaze of muzzle flashes and gun smoke. The creature reeled, dropping to one knee. Shannon glanced at Graham. That much silver should have put it down to stay but it was still very much alive.

"Something is powering it," Graham told him.

"S-H-A-N-N-O-N!" the monster roared as it got to its feet.

He and Graham were desperately trying to reload as Graham's control over their horses faltered. The animals went crazy, rearing and bucking underneath them. Graham toppled to the ground first. Shannon held on a bit longer before he too was thrown. The creature's claws latched onto one of the horses as it lifted the beast into the air above its head and slammed it down on Shannon like a weapon. Shannon began to transform into his monster form out of desperation. The other horse raced away, happy to be free of them all.

Graham had managed to load two rounds into his Colt's cylinder. He flipped the gun closed and raised it as the monster's face. "Die you. . ." he started but the monster again moved nearly as fast as Zed, dodging Graham's first shot as it closed in on him. One of its hands closed over Graham's own, crushing it and the pistol it held. Its other closed over Graham's head. The creature's long, clawed fingers sunk through Graham's skull into his brain. Graham's eyes bugged and blood rolled down over his cheeks. Graham's body twitched where it lay as the thing turned towards Shannon.

Shannon was now totally wolfed out. His eight-foot-tall, white-haired body hunched and ready to meet the monster. A gust of wind swept through the space between them. Zed was there in human form, moving faster than Shannon had ever seen before. Zed ripped Sarah's daggers from the creature's chest. He raced around the monster in circles, slashing and hacking at its hide with the two blades. Geysers of blood sprayed in every direction. When Zed skidded to a halt, there wasn't enough of the creature left standing to recognize it as a living thing. What remained of its ravaged and hacked form toppled over to lay still at Zed's feet.

"Graham!" Shannon heard Sarah yelling. She ran to where Graham was sprawled in the dirt, his head resting in a pool of his own blood, and fell to her knees beside his corpse.

Zed met Shannon's eyes. "I wasn't fast enough, was I?"

"You saved me, Zed," was the only answer Shannon could give.

* * *

As the sun rose, Sarah, Yule, Zed, and Shannon stood over Graham's hastily made grave.

"Somebody should say something," Yule said in what passed for a whisper for him. It was still loud enough for all of them to hear. The family was all in human form and dressed. Dark bruises covered Yule's skin and Sarah's head was wrapped in makeshift bandage underneath her hat. Sprigs of what was left of her hair poked through from underneath its edges.

Zed held his hat in his hands in front of him. "Graham was the best liar I ever knew but once in a while he told the truth too when it really mattered."

Sarah body shook with sobs. "I'm sorry, Mom," she said, then turned to walk away. Shannon knew she'd promised their mother she'd take care of Graham and watch out for him but there was nothing more she could have done try to save him. Yule seemed satisfied with their words and lumbered after her.

"Gonna be tough on her," Shannon commented.

"What do you care?" Zed asked. "You left us, broke her heart. We weren't good enough for you then, Shannon. Who could honestly expect you to care now?"

Zeds words cut him to the quick.

"Let's finish this mess with Samuel," Zed said and followed the others.

Shannon stood at Graham's grave alone.

* * *

"That's him for sure," Zed told Shannon. From the slight hill they stood on they could see a large force, moving on foot in the distance.

"He's heading northeast. Should bring him right to us," Shannon said.

"How many of them do you reckon there are?" Zed asked.

"Too many," Sarah told them as she and Yule came up the hill. "At least sixty, I'd say, maybe more. You boys got a plan?"

"Shoot 'em all until they're dead?" Zed shrugged.

Shannon saw the glare she gave Zed and was glad he wasn't him.

"Graham was usually the one with the plan," Zed frowned. "I am open to suggestions."

"That thing that attacked us," Shannon spoke up, "It knew my name. I was the one it wanted. Maybe Samuel wants me for some reason."

"I know what you're thinking, Shannon," Sarah said, "but I don't think Samuel sent the creature."

"You got a better plan?" Shannon challenged her.

"I do," Zed laughed, "but ya'll ain't gonna like it any better."

* * *

Zed stepped into the road from one of the many rocks littering the desert valley. The stunned look on Samuel's face was priceless. The men on both sides of Samuel went for their guns as those behind them came to a sudden stop.

"No!" Samuel screamed, "Hold your fire! There are four more of them. Watch for them," he warned his men.

Zed and Samuel stared at each other.

"Good to see you, Samuel," Zed smiled, making no move to approach his brother.

"Where's the rest of the family, Zed?" Samuel asked.

"Graham's dead," Zed told him.

"The man in white?" Samuel growled, asking the question as if he were talking to himself.

"Who?" Zed asked.

"What do you want, Zed?" Samuel changed the subject though he was clearly shocked by the news of Graham's death.

"Oh, I figure you know exactly why I'm here, brother." Zed took a count of the men he faced. In addition to the two Colts on his hips, he was packing two more tucked under his belt against his back. "Don't suppose you want to make this easy and surrender, do you?"

"I know how fast you are Zed but not even you can hope to survive this kind of standoff."

"You know, Samuel, before he died, Graham and I had ourselves a talk about the mistake of underestimating things. Pray I kill you because if Sarah gets her hands on you after what you did to Graham. . ." Zed let his words trail off.

"What I am doing is right, Zed. The humans don't deserve this world. They're weak and misguided. Think for a second about what we could accomplish if we all worked together like in the old days. It doesn't have to be this way."

Zed grinned, flashing razored teeth below his sallow eyes. "You ain't half the talker Graham was. He might have sold me on this crap you're planning but you. . .you're just sick, mate."

As Samuel's men raised their rifles and shotguns, Zed was already in motion. He ran straight at them, drawing the two pistols from behind his back. His first shot caught the man next to Samuel in the forehead, knocking him from his feet. The second splattered the brains of a man leveling a Winchester at him. His third struck a man with his Colt halfway out of its holster in the arm causing the man to fling the gun away as he drew it. His fourth dropped a bearded man with a shotgun. His next two shots streaked towards Samuel but his brother was ready for them. A bluish green shield of some kind glimmered around Samuel as the bullets struck it and bounced harmlessly away. Zed emptied the two Colts, watching Samuel turn tail and run as his men continued to fall around him. As Zed drew his second set of Colts, seven of Samuel's men were dead and two others wounded. Zed was laughing like the devil himself as he opened fire again. Bullets flew at him in slow motion. He ducked one, sidestepped another, fired a shot of his own taking down a blond teenager with a shot that buried itself in the young man's heart. Zed flipped through the air over another wave of bullets as they came at him. He landed, squatting, as his Colts blazed. Samuel's men were beginning to realize their fellow wolves weren't getting up.

"He's using silver bullets!" someone screamed before one of Zed's rounds entered his open mouth and blew out the backside of his skull. The man's body fell, twitching, into the sand. More men moved forward to take the place of those who had fallen. The bullets were so many now that Zed couldn't dodge them all. A Winchester round blew out his right knee and then it was over. His body shook and danced as he was riddled with bullets. At last, he slumped to the ground still trying to fight until a round from a Colt split open his head like an overripe melon.

Zed's diversion had worked perfectly. Yule rose up on top of a rock on the men's left flank, his Gatling gun thundering. He held the huge gun with one hand, squeezing its trigger, as his other hand spun the weapon's crank. Yule swept its stream of fire over Samuel's men cutting them to pieces where they stood. Shannon and Sarah came at the men from their other flank. Sarah carried two pistols, firing one then the other as she ran towards them. Shannon stood his ground empting a Winchester into their ranks.

"Change!" Samuel was yelling, "Change and overrun them before they kill us all!"

As Samuel's men became wolves and charged at Yule, the giant flung his Gatling gun like a spear with such brute force it that it sank into and through the chest of the lead monster. Shannon watched the giant meet four of Samuel's remaining men, head on. The family's plan had reduced the number of Samuel's force to less than two dozen. Those were odds Shannon could live with. His Winchester hit the sand as he switched to his Colts. A seven-foot-tall wolf on two legs came roaring at him. He put three rounds into its gut as he charged forward, hunting for Samuel amid the chaos. He jumped over The Changed's corpse, whipping one of his Colts around to fire point blank into the snarling teeth of another one of Samuel's men. He saw Sarah taking on three of the monster wolves at once. Her daggers were in her hands. She moved with a natural grace as she danced among them, ducking their blows to land ones of her own.

Shannon spotted Samuel and two of his men, still in human form, as they were hightailing it southward, the battle abandoned. Shannon jumped through the air, shifting into his wolf form before he landed on all fours and shot after them like a bullet.

"Yeehah!" he heard Zed scream as his little brother leapt up, finally healed from his numerous wounds, to join Sarah and Yule in finishing up the last of Samuel's foot soldiers. None of Samuel's men had been using silver bullets, just as Zed had guessed when he came up with his crazy plan. The sound of his Colts reminded Shannon of Yule's Gatling gun.

As Shannon caught up to Samuel, the two lackeys with his brother moved to block his path. Shannon crippled one, shifting into his two-legged form to rake his claws upwards through the man's groin. The man collapsed, howling in pain. The other man began to transform but Shannon clawed his face, taking out one of his eyes, and sent him sprawling into the sand.

Samuel made a show of applauding him. "Bravo!"

Shannon's head snapped around to glare at him. "Samuel," Shannon growled, the sides of his mouth quivering with anger, "your army is dead."

"Indeed. I would have expected no less from our family. I can always start again."

"You're a fool if you think you're leaving here alive. Your magic isn't going to save you."

"You're right. This time I thought I would take a much more hands-on approach." Samuel shrugged off his black robe as white fur grew on his skin. "The power of the Wendigo," he said, his voice like the screaming wind, "is all I need."

Shannon watched his brother's transformation in horror. The thing Samuel became was no wolf. It stood twelve feet tall, its muscles so large and thick Shannon could see through the dense, white hair now covering Samuel's body. The thing had the general shape of a man with a mane of hair about its head and a whip-like tail that dangled between its legs. The claws on its hands were the size of daggers. Its silver eyes burned with the heat of a furnace. Shannon retreated a step as Samuel spoke again, "What's the matter, brother? Am I not beautiful?"

"You're an abomination," Shannon heard Sarah say as she joined him.. Yule was with her in his monster form.

"You may be big but I am still the strongest," Yule roared.

"Try me, Yule." Samuel motioned to them with his long fingers, waving them forward.

Yule bared his teeth and rushed at Samuel. Samuel met him head on, the two titans crashing into each other like runaway locomotives. Yule's claws ripped at Samuel, drawing blood. One of Samuel's huge, paw like hands closed on Yule's head and smashed him, face first, into the sand. Yule struggled against the grip as Samuel held him there, pinned to the ground. A smile stretched over Samuel's black lips. "Next?" he laughed.

Sarah and Shannon moved together. Sarah going in on Samuel's left, slashing at the arm that held Yule with her silver daggers. Shannon came in from the right and leapt onto Samuel, his claws sinking into the flesh of his chest, holding him there. Shannon ripped one hand free of Samuel's skin, spraying blood and taking a chunk of him with it in the process, as he tried to rake at his brother's face. Samuel's claws slid into Yule's brains, killing him, as he swung Yule's body at Sarah like a club. Sarah dodged, rolling away. Samuel's other hand plucked Shannon off of him and tossed Shannon aside like a troublesome insect. A cloud of dust appeared on the horizon, then Zed was standing in front of Samuel, a pair of six-guns in his hands. Zed opened up on Samuel. Round after round pelted Samuel, causing him to stumble. Sarah took advantage of Samuel's surprise and pain, leaping onto his back.

"You killed Graham!" she howled as her daggers met beneath Samuel's chin and slit his throat. She slid back to the ground. Blood poured over the white hair of Samuel's chest from the long gash stretching from one side of his throat to the other. He made a sickening, gargling noise as he tried to say something.

With a running start, Shannon slammed into him, toppling him over. Shannon sat atop his massive chest, slashing at Samuel wildly with his claws until they were both drenched in red and Samuel lay still beneath him.

"Shannon!" Sarah yelled, "That's enough! He's dead!"

"He killed Kira!" Shannon shouted and started tearing away at Samuel again.

"Whoa, brother," Zed swooped in to pin Shannon's arms behind his head, restraining him, "let it go."

A wounded man, missing most of the side of his face, including his right eye, came staggering towards them. He was clearly one of the Changed who had survived. He collapsed beside Samuel's corpse. "How could you?" the man asked with tears flowing from his remaining eye. "He was your brother."

"He killed my wife," Shannon answered. "The bastard got what he deserved."

The man looked at him. "You're him, ain't ya? Shannon? Samuel didn't kill your wife. The man in white did that. I overheard him telling Samuel that was the only way he could make sure you would come with the others. Samuel was furious about it but it had already been done. That wasn't too long before the man in white and my boss parted ways."

"Who the heck are you?" Zed asked.

"My name is Ed," the man told them, "Samuel was my father."

Shannon stared at Ed, his eyes going wide. He could see the resemblance now. Tiny flakes of silver floated in the man's remaining eye, swirling around like leaves in the breeze.

"Please," Ed begged, "Please just go and let me die with him in peace."

"Come on, Shannon." Zed helped him to his feet.

Shannon shook Zed's hands off of him. "Wait! Who is this man in white?"

Ed couldn't answer him. Ed had slumped onto Samuel's corpse and passed on to join his father in the next life.

* * *

The family stood over Yule's grave. There were only three of them left. Sarah placed a single flower on the top of the freshly-packed dirt and backed away.

"I can't believe Yule's gone." Zed wiped at his eyes, pretending he had something in them but Shannon knew better.

"There's been too much death," Sarah agreed. Shannon said nothing.

"I'm gonna miss the big idiot," Zed admitted.

"What now?" Sarah asked.

"It's not over," Shannon found the strength to say aloud. "It won't be until I find this man in white and make him pay." He saw Zed frowning.

"It's over for me, Shannon. I think I'd like to see what life is like without having to watch your back."

"Good for you, Zed," Sarah smiled. "Graham was worth a fortune. Go claim it and start over."

Zed grinned, "I think I just might."

"Sarah," Shannon looked at her, "Come with me."

"If you had asked me a few years ago Shannon, I would have followed you anywhere." She shook her head sadly. "But not this time. I've got some things to sort out myself."

"Guess this is goodbye then, huh?" Shannon asked.

"For now," Sarah nodded. "Come find me when you're done chasing ghosts. We'll talk."

Sarah hugged them both and darted away towards the setting sun.

"Have I told you you're an idiot lately?" Zed smiled, kicking at the ground with the tip of his boot. "Even if you find this man in white, killing him isn't going to bring Kira back from the dead."

"I know," Shannon nodded, "but I need to do this, Zed."

"God be with you, brother," Zed told him, then he was gone, leaving a cloud of dust in his wake. Shannon stood at Yule's grave for a moment longer then slung a Winchester loaded with silver bullets onto his shoulder and started his long trek east. He couldn't explain it but he knew that was where the man in white had gone. It was like there was a voice in his head, calling him to North Carolina. It didn't matter. One way or another, he would find the man in white and when he did, it would all be over.

POSTSCRIPT

THE SCENT OF THE MAN IN WHITE WAS EVERYWHERE. It was ancient, powerful, and evil. Shannon hid behind the thick trunk of a tree, his Winchester ready in his hands. The voice in his head had been right about the man in white being here in North Carolina. Shannon had found his trail easily once he reached the south. He was somewhere very, very close now, here in these woods. The moon was bright and full in the sky above. Shannon soaked in its rays, enjoying their feel on his skin. The very air seemed be charged with some kind energy. Shannon had never felt anything like it before.

Something moved in the woods nearby. Whatever it was, it was far too big to be the man in white. Shannon heard it breaking tree limbs as it tore its way through the woods at a speed impossible for a normal man. As it drew closer to his position, he realized it was coming for him.

Shannon spun from behind the tree into the thing's path. His eyes bugged as he saw the monster approaching him. It was huge. The thing stood over ten feet tall and was covered head to toe in mangy, matted hair. It ran on two legs, with long lopping strides, and its arms were impossibly long.

His Winchester thundered as he put a round into its chest. The bullet didn't even slow it down. It was on him before he could manage another shot. One of its huge hands slammed into him, crunching bone, and flinging him backwards to bounce off a tree behind him.

Blood poured from Shannon's nose as the damage to his face began to heal. Whatever the thing was, it wasn't supernatural or he wouldn't be regenerating. He took comfort in that fact as the thing reared its head back in a roar so loud it echoed throughout the woods.

Suddenly, both he and the monster were forced to cover their eyes as the night lit up with an explosion of light. When it was over, a man dressed in a long, gray coat and some kind of military looking uniform lay in the grass several feet from them. The monster turned its attention to the man, moving towards him with a snarl on its lips.

Shannon sprang onto the monster's back as claws grew from his fingertips. His claws tore into its flesh as he climbed its shoulders to get at its neck. The monster roared again, trying to shake him off. It reached for him but couldn't quite get a hold on him. Shannon's teeth became razors. Leaning in as he avoided one of its groping hands, Shannon bit into the side of its neck and ripped away a chunk of meat, sending geysers of blood spraying over him and into the night air. He leapt away as the monster stumbled, staggering around, until it fell over.

The man in the military uniform had gotten to his feet and stood watching it all. In a heavy German accent he said, *"Mein Gott,* you're a werewolf and that. . . That was a... *unglaublich*...a Sasquatch." He waved at the corpse of the monster.

Shannon advanced on him, his teeth bared between his blood smeared lips, yet the man didn't appear to be frightened at all.

"Are you the one who has brought me here?" the man in the military uniform asked. "The one I can feel?"

"What?" Shannon growled. "What do you mean feel?"

"My name is Merrick," the man said, stepping forward to extend his hand as if he had somehow looked inside Shannon's mind and found the answers to his questions there. "I think, *mein freund*, we've got some hunting to do."

PART THREE

Once Upon a Bloody Twilight

LIEUTENANT JENKINS FELT SICK. HE DID HIS BEST TO hide it and keep up his professional demeanor. Jenkins was no stranger to death. He had seen his friends die next to him as bullets tore their guts apart and settlers on their way to a new home scalped. This though was something different. The bodies that lay in the dirt of the small clearing had been savaged. Very few of them were completely intact. Pieces of what once were human beings lay scattered everywhere. The soil and grass were drenched with blood. Whatever had happened here taken place recently, the blood from the bodies was still congealing. Lieutenant Jenkins forced himself to stop staring at the carnage and looked up at the sky. It would be getting dark soon. The sun was slowly creeping behind the distant mountains. A shudder he couldn't stop ran through him.

"You okay sir?" Hyatt asked.

"Fine," Jenkins lied, turning to face the private. Hyatt was a wide-eyed kid who had only joined up recently. He was strong and bright though so if he lived long enough, Jenkins imagined Hyatt had a good career ahead of him.

Their squad had been dispatched to aid Sheriff Wiggins' posse which had set out from Clarksville. Several of the townsfolk there had been killed in the last few days and Wiggins had sent work asking for help in finding out who was responsible for the attacks on the town. Captain Everett, Jenkins' superior, feared that it was Indians from the horrific details about the state of the bodies of those who had been found dead in the letter Wiggins had sent. He had told Jenkins to pick out a squad and ride out to meet up with Wiggins' posse at once. Their hurried flight had brought them here to what once appeared to be the posse's camp where Wiggins had stopped to wait for their arrival before heading deeper into the woods surrounding the clearing.

Jenkins' squad consisted for himself and five soldiers he had hand-picked for the job. Among them were Hyatt who was still so green he almost seemed to be too young to carry a rifle, Hall, the party's sharp shooter, Charles and Johnson, tough veterans who were the squad's muscle and the scars to prove they were as hardened as they claimed to be, and Dave. Dave was the best pistolier Jenkins had ever seen and one heck of a tracker to boot. They were his men and he had believed they were up to dealing with anything that they could possibly run into and come out of it alive. He had believed that at least until they had seen the tendrils of smoke rising into the sky that had lead them to this camp and found what was left of Sheriff Wiggins' posse. As badly as some of the bodies were torn up, it was hard to tell exactly how many men had made up the sheriff's party but his best guess put the number at fifteen.

Charles and Johnson had taken up defensive positions at the edges of the clearing and were keeping an eye in case whatever killed Sheriff Wiggins' party was still nearby. Hall was leaning against a tree staring at the carnage in the clearing, his rifle held in his hands. Dave was following him around like a puppy having decided to personally take on the task of making sure that he stayed alive. Lieutenant Jenkins was glad to have Dave near and looking out for him but at the same time was annoyed by the pistolier shadowing him so closely.

Lieutenant Jenkins knew that Dave had seen even more action than he had. He was surprised when Dave spoke up to ask, "What do you think happened here sir?"

He didn't have an answer. Jenkins shrugged and then shook his head. "Indians maybe?"

Dave shot him a look that told Jenkins the pistolier knew dang blasted well that even Indians weren't capable of this sort of desecration and savagery.

Rolling up a cigarette, Dave lit it, taking a long drag. "Looks more like the work of some kind of animal to me sir. Them bodies have bit marks on them."

Lieutenant Jenkins wanted to tell Dave not to remind him of that fact but it was true. The bodies of Sheriff Wiggins' posse weren't just torn up. They looked to have been eaten on too as if something had paused to feast on them after slaughtering them.

"At least they were able to put up a fight," Hyatt commented.

There were spent rifle casings in the dirt and several of the men had been able to draw their pistols for whatever good it had done them. Clearly they had tried to fight back against whatever had come at them. There was no sign of bodies that didn't appear to belong to the posse though.

"Whoever hit them, hit them so hard and fast all this . . ." Dave gestured at the bodies strewn about the clearing, "It was over in a matter of minutes if that long. I suggest we get out of here before night fall sir. We don't have the men to defend this place. It's too open and any one coming at us has the trees to use for cover. If they're good, they could be on top of us before we even knew they were there."

"We can't just leave these men like this . . ." Hyatt protested.

Before Lieutenant Jenkins could answer, Dave said, "They're dead boy and odds are we'll be joining them in Hell if we stay here any longer than we have to. Whoever did this could be watching us right now for all we know."

"Dave's right," Lieutenant Jenkins told Hyatt. "Our priority has to be finding somewhere we can hunker down before it gets dark."

They had tied their horses on the south side of the clearing where a well-traveled trail led into it. The animal seemed as uneasy as his men were as Lieutenant Jenkins started towards them.

"Riders coming in!" Charles yelled from his position beyond where the horses were tied.

Lieutenant Jenkins broke into a run with Dave and Hyatt on his heels heading to meet whoever was coming up the trail. His right hand slipped his pistol free of the holster on his belt as he leaped over the ravaged torso of a posse member's body that was in his path. Johnson remained where he was covering the clearing's far side.

"Two of them sir," Charles said gesturing down the trail.

Lieutenant Jenkins saw the riders. One appeared to be a thin, young man with hawk like eyes and the other was a . . . woman. Jenkins blinked in surprise as she came better into view. She wore the clothes of a gun-fighter and long red hair spilled over her shoulders from beneath her hat. There was something strapped to her back but it didn't appear to be a rifle. Jenkins squinted in the dying rays of the sun trying to make it out. It looked to be a sword of some kind.

The riders moved at a slow and steady pace and rode with a confidence, or perhaps arrogance, that told Lieutenant Jenkins they were trouble waiting to happen.

"Stop where you are!" Lieutenant Jenkins shouted at them while they were still several yards out. The pistol he clutched in his hand was leveled at them as he spoke. Hyatt and Charles had their rifles aimed at the riders as well. Though he couldn't see Hall any longer, he would wager that the sharp shooter had his sights on the riders too. Dave's pistols remained in their holsters but his hands were poised over them.

"Evening Lieutenant," the thin man purred at him apparently seeing the rank bars Jenkins wore on his uniform. "We ain't looking for any trouble."

Lieutenant Jenkins considered ordering them to turn around and head back the way they had come but decided that would be a bad idea. The two of them could easily give the appearance of doing and then double back after they were out of sight. His gut told him that these two weren't the killer or killers he was after but it also told him that they were as dangerous as concealed viper waiting to strike.

"What y'all doing out here?" Dave asked. "These woods ain't no place for decent folks."

"Likely the same thing you are," the woman said. "We've got papers I'd be glad to show you if you wouldn't mind lowering your guns."

"Papers?" Lieutenant Jenkins asked still trying to make sense of everything. It was all happening so fast.

"We were hired by the folks over in Dobson," the thin man answered. "Been some killings over there and we're on the trail of the gent responsible for them."

Dobson was the next closest town to Clarksville. It lay just north and west of Fort Pendergrast where he and his men had ridden from. The distance between the two wasn't that great. Lieutenant Jenkins wondered if the attacks in Clarksville were the work of the same person the riders claimed to be after. He gestured for his men to lower their weapons as the woman reached under her coat to produce a crumpled up sheet of paper. Dave kept the riders covered as the two of them dismounted.

The woman walked up to him handing him the paper. Lieutenant Jenkins struggled to read it in the dying light but it looked to be real and in perfect order.

"So the two of you are bounty hunters or something?" Lieutenant Jenkins asked.

"Or something," the thin man grinned. "I'm Zek and this here is my sister, Sarah."

"Lieutenant Jenkins," he said passing the paper back to Sarah. She took it and tucked it away inside her jacket again.

They all stood in an uneasy silence for a moment before Lieutenant Jenkins spoke again. "Look . . ." he started.

Zek snorted. "You can spare us the bit about this being official business lieutenant. We're here to do a job just like you are and you ain't gonna stop us."

"I think it would be best if we worked together don't you Lieutenant?" Sarah smiled at him.

As she did so, Lieutenant Jenkins noticed that was something that wasn't quite right about her teeth. Her incisors seemed just slightly overly long somehow. That fact did nothing to detract from her beauty though. The curves of his body made his heart race inside his chest and he felt sweat beading up on his skin as he looked into her deep green eyes.

"Yes," he answered. "Perhaps that would be best."

"Sir?" Dave's head jerked around at him.

"Their papers are in order Dave," Lieutenant Jenkins assured the pistolier. "They have as much right to be here as we do."

"Yes sir," Dave grunted clearly unhappy with the situation.

Lieutenant Jenkins turned his attention back to Zek and Sarah. "I don't suppose you have any information about the killer we're all after that would be helpful do you?"

Zek laughed. Lieutenant Jenkins saw Sarah shot him a stern look silencing him.

"We know exactly what we're after Lieutenant," Sarah answered. "And it's close by. I can smell it from here."

"That so?" Dave challenged the red head.

"Hold up," Lieutenant Jenkins interrupted. "What do you mean *it?*"

"The thing you're after Lieutenant . . ." Zek continued to grin at him. "It ain't human in the slightest."

"You're saying an animal did this?" Lieutenant Jenkins gawked at Zek in disbelief.

"Of a sorts I suppose," Sarah nodded. "But not the type of animal you're thinking of."

"You two need to start making some sense and fast," Dave warned Zek and Sarah. "We don't got time for all this yakking. The sun's almost down and we're all still just standing here like a bunch of fools asking to meet our maker."

Johnson's scream rang out in the night echoing amid the trees. Lieutenant Jenkins and his men whirled about to look in the direction it had come from. The scream was followed by the crack of Hall's rifle. Zek and Sarah were already on the move though sprinting across the clearing. Sarah unsheathed the sword she carried on her back as she ran. It looked oriental but Lieutenant Jenkins couldn't remember what it was called though he had seen it's like before in books he had read from his father's library back home before he had enlisted.

The *thing*, there was no other word for it, that burst from the trees where Johnson had been standing watch was monstrous. It had the overall shape of a man and wore ragged, blood stained clothes but that was where its resemblance to anything human ended. Its skin was scaled like a reptile's and huge leathery wings unfolded to protrude from behind its shoulders. The thing's eyes burned in the dim light of the falling night like the flames of a raging campfire. Its fingers were tipped long claws that were curved like those of a cat. And the shriek the thing gave as it charged forward chilled Lieutenant Jenkins to the depths of his very soul. Hall's shot had struck it in the center of its chest. Putrid, black fluid bubbled from the wound like molasses from the trunk of a tree.

Zek was knocked from his feet as the creature increased its speed, plowing into him. Sarah's sword swung at the thing. Its blade sunk into and through the creature's side spraying black blood into the air. The creature screeched in pain but didn't falter. One of its hands lashed out at Sarah, backhanding her with enough force to send her flying. She thudded onto the ground several yards from where the creature stood.

Lieutenant Jenkins' men joined the battle. Hall's rifle coughed again this time putting a bullet directly into the creature's skull between its eyes. Its head snapped back on its neck from the impact and the same black blood spurted from the hole the bullet had punched in the front of its skull but the creature refused to die. It jumped into the air, taking flight, soaring upwards at an incredible speed. The creature shifted its course and dove at Hall. The sharp shooter cried out as the creature came at him. His cry was silenced as a single swipe of its claws reduced his face to a mass mangled meat.

Dave's pistols had left their holsters. They thundered in rapid succession as the pistolier emptied them into the creature drawing its attention. Charles stepped between Dave and the creature at the last possible second, his rifle up and aimed at the creature's screeching mouth. Charles didn't have time to fire though. The creature batted the rifle from his grasp as its other hand plunged into his stomach. It emerged pulling red slicked, purple strands of intestines out with it. Charles' scream was sickening thing to hear as he stared down at handful of his own entrails that the creature clutched. The creature used them to yank Charles forward. Its head came forward and the razor like teeth that filled its mouth crunched into the bone of Charles' head. Charles' body twitched as the creature grabbed it and held him in place while it took another bite out of him before looking up at Lieutenant Jenkins with its glowing, burning eyes.

Dave was reloading as fast as he could as Hyatt came at the monster from behind. The creature sensed the young man's approach and let Charles' corpse drop to the dirt as it spun about. Hyatt fired his rifle pointed blank into the creature. It grunted at the impact of the bullet that slammed into it but otherwise ignored the damage Hyatt's bullet had done to its ribs. It snatched Hyatt by the arms and jerked them free of his body. Hyatt wailed, blood spraying from where his arms had connected to his shoulders, as the creature brought up a foot to kick him in the chest. Hyatt's ribcage shattered, blood like vomit spewing up out of his mouth, as he was sent flying towards the edge of the clearing. The creature turned its attention to Dave again just as the pistolier finished loading one of his weapons and flipped its chamber closed. Dave's eyes went wide and Lieutenant Jenkins so that even as fast as Dave was that the pistolier wasn't going to have the time to get off a shot. The creature's claws raked across Dave's neck ending the pistolier's life before Lieutenant Jenkins could even shout a warning.

"Hey! Leave those humans alone!" Lieutenant Jenkins heard Sarah shout at the creature. Its head jerked around in her direction.

The creature gave a high-pitched shriek and raced towards her. Sarah stood her ground. Her eyes were glowing now like the creature's. As the creature moved towards her, something else jumped to intercept it. The thing that tackled the creature wore Zek's clothes but it wasn't a man. It more closely resembled a wolf that stood on two legs. The wolf's claws slashed at the creature time and time again so fast that they were little more than a blur to Lieutenant Jenkins' eyes. They tore huge chunks of flesh from the creature with each blow. The creature lay on in the dirt at the center of a pool its own black blood as the wolf thing rose and backed away from it.

"Finish it Sarah," the wolf thing snarled in a distorted version of Zek's voice.

Sarah moved forward to bring the blade of her sword down severing the creature's head from its shoulders. The fires raging in the creature's eyes went dark as its head bounced away from its body.

Lieutenant Jenkins found himself alone in the clearing with Sarah and the man-wolf that had spoken with Zek's voice.

"It's over," Sarah said, sounding relieved.

"Yep," the wolf said and then nodded in his direction. "I guess the question now is what do we do with him?"

Lieutenant Jenkins stared at Sarah and the wolf. He heard his own stammering voice plead, "P-p-please don't kill me."

"We don t have to deal with him Zek," Sarah giggled. "Nobody's going to believe a word he says about any of this and you know it. The job's done and that's all that matters. "

The wolf in the clothes of a man grunted his agreement and started for where the two of them had left their horses. Sarah picked up the creature's head by the mangy hair atop its malformed head and carried it with her as she started after the wolf. She paused to glance back over her shoulder.

"It was good meeting you Lieutenant," Sarah smirked at him. "You take care of yourself now."

Lieutenant Jenkins watched her join the wolf that had somehow become Zek again at the horses. The two of them rode off into the night without another word. Lieutenant Jenkins stood there frozen with fear long after they were gone.

Town Killer

ZED PUSHED THE BIKE'S ENGINE TO ITS LIMITS, BAR-reling down the winding mountain road. The town of Canton came into view ahead of him. It was one of those rare, small, out-of-the-way places where everyone knew everyone and the entire population consisted of only a few hundred, if his intel was correct. He'd traveled across half the country to get here. Zed remembered a time when such a trip would have taken far longer. He missed the old days. Things were much simpler back then.

Easing off the accelerator, he slowed the bike as the edge of town approached. The last thing he needed was some hick cop trying to ticket him. He cruised into the town's main street. It was too early on a Sunday for many folks to be up and about yet. Spotting the local diner, Zed pulled over into its parking lot. There were a few cars in the lot as he parked his bike and sauntered into the diner. Every head in the place turned to stare at him as he entered. He took off his biker's helmet, letting gray hair spill onto the shoulders of his leather jacket.

"Morning," he said to the thin, dark-haired waitress who met him as he took a seat in one of the booths.

"Welcome to Clyde's," she said, doing her best to feign a cheerful tone. "What can I get you?"

"Coffee. Black. Three of them," he told her.

"Three?" she asked, frowning at the odd request. "You expecting company?"

Zed shook his head. "Been a long ride and I ain't as fast as I used to be," he answered honestly.

The young waitress nodded, "Whatever you say, mister."

He watched her head off to fetch his coffee, enjoying the view of her bottom and long legs in the short skirt she wore as she moved. The other patrons had returned their attention to their meals and conversations, or at least they pretended to. He knew better. Zed stunk to high heaven from his arduous ride to get here. If they couldn't smell him then they were even dumber than they all looked. He could feel the twin, customized Glocks holstered and hidden beneath his thick leather jacket pressing into him. Doing a quick head count of those in the diner, he came up with seventeen, counting the two waitresses and the cook in the back. Things would be getting real hairy soon.

The waitress returned with his coffees, placing them on the table before him. He downed the first cup, ignoring the burn from its heat. The waitress loomed over him.

"Mind if I ask what brings you to Canton, mister? Ain't much going on here this time of year with all the ski resorts and such closed up for the summer."

"I ain't no tourist," Zed said, sipping on his second cup of coffee.

She was pushing hard, trying to figure him out. These folks wouldn't want to play their hand unless they were sure he was the kind of trouble he smelt like. Zed looked up into her green eyes and said, "I heard there were some wolves in these parts. That true?"

"Wolves?" the young waitress asked. "Where did you hear that from?"

Zed laughed. "Didn't have to hear it. I can smell y'all right plain."

The waitress's eyes flashed red. "He's a hunter!" she screamed.

The others in the diner began getting to their feet. He could smell the fear and hate in them as one huge man in a trucker's cap and flannel shirt yelled, "Get the bastard!"

Zed moved so fast his hands were a blur, drawing his Glocks. His expression still calm, he opened up on the crowd from where he sat. The waitress died first, catching a round in her temple that sent her careening backwards to sprawl on the floor. Each of Zed's first shots ended a life. Five more of the crowd were dead before they could even begin to try to reach him. Zed's Glocks were firing so fast they sounded like machine guns. The large man in flannel took a round that pierced his cheek, shattering teeth, on its path up into his brain. In seconds, everyone in the diner except for Zed and the cook in the back were dead or prone, bleeding out, on the diner's floor. That cook was going to be a problem, Zed figured. He left his booth, moving to the center of the diner where he could see into the kitchen area more clearly. There was no sign of the cook. Either he'd gone for a weapon or transformed and was waiting for the right moment to pounce. The Changed were usually too proud to run. They saw themselves as equals to their Pure Blood kindred like himself.

Zed knew he didn't have much time. Even in a small town like Canton, gunfire in the amount that had just occurred would bring the authorities running. Zed waited though, letting the cook make the first move. He didn't have to wait long. An eight-foot-tall, half-wolf creature covered in black hair from head to toe came tearing through the kitchen door at him with blazing red eyes and a snarling face. As fast as the monster was, Zed was faster. He calmly put a bullet in its forehead. Blood sprayed from the lethal wound as the huge beast toppled forward from its own momentum, rolling across the floor to come to a stop at his feet. Zed could hear the sound of sirens wailing in the distance. He thought for a second about running but decided to stand his ground. If this whole town was truly populated by the Changed, he'd have to kill the officers eventually anyway. Why not let them come to him?

Two cars with flashing blue lights whipped into the diner's parking area. In their hurry, one of them clipped his bike, sending it clattering over onto the pavement. Zed cursed, walking out to meet the officers. They had no way of knowing that there was a pure blood hunter in town much less one with silver bullets. The advantage was his. Two officers emerged from the first car. Another climbed out of the second. All of them had their guns drawn and held ready. The wind carried their scent to him and told Zed all he needed to know.

"Stop right there!" one of the cops ordered him. "Drop those guns, mister!"

Zed answered the warning with his Glocks. The first two officers were dead before they even knew what was happening. The last one managed to get off a shot of his own. Zed watched the bullet coming towards him in slow motion and easily stepped from its path. The last officer's head exploded in a rain of gore and bone fragments as Zed's Glocks boomed again. He walked over to the corpse of the closest cop and checked the dead man's pistol. The bullets inside were standard issue. That meant the cops were just for show. The town's real protectors were out there somewhere still. Every tribe of the Changed had an alpha male and usually a small number of seconds who watched over the others and carried out his will. Zed reloaded his Glocks with fresh mags and holstered them. Not even a pureblood like himself could fight an entire town of lesser wolves. What he needed to do was find the Alpha. With him gone, the others would scatter and he could hunt them down one by one at his leisure. Zed sniffed the air searching for the strongest wolf scent he could find and then took off after it to the south. In seconds, his speed was pushing two hundred miles an hour.

The scent led him to the Wally World super center on the far side of town. The air stank of the Alpha's scent. The super center was a massive, twenty-four hour establishment, right off the interstate. It was a place for tourists and passing travelers. Even on a Sunday morning in the off season, there were at least fifty cars in its lot. Thankfully, he had chosen to stop short of its actual parking lot and stood among the trees of a close by hill looking down into it. There were humans here. Taking out the Alpha without endangering them or revealing the existence of wolves among them wasn't going to be easy. He wished Sarah was with him. His sister always had a plan in situations like this. His style was a bit more "go in guns blazing" and that was not an option at the moment. Zed cleaned himself up as best he could and checked over his appearance. Maybe he'd be lucky enough that the Alpha was still unaware of his presence in the town, but that was unlikely. If nothing else, odds were the Alpha could smell the scent of a pureblood close by and knew death had come into his little dominion.

Zed strolled down the hill and across the parking lot. He didn't need his nose to tell him the door greeter was a wolf. The elderly man in the store's trademark blue vest scowled at him as he entered. Zed headed straight for the back of the store. Shoving open two large doors marked "employees only," he stepped into the stockroom/loading area. A huge man in expensive looking clothes flanked by four other men in blue vests waited on him there.

"Who are you?" the big man asked.

Zed read his manager's badge. "Well, Larry, I'm Zed Farr."

The lesser wolves went pale but the big man kept a semblance of composure.

"Farr," he spat, "You're a murder and a traitor to our race."

"What race would that be? From where I'm standing, you don't look to be wolf or man," Zed said. He knew his words were the greatest insult he could give to one of the Changed. The Changed thought of themselves as real wolves, though in truth they weren't. They were nothing more than victims of a virus that gave them a semblance of what the pure-bloods were capable of.

"Kill him!" The big man yelled to his lackeys.

The four men rushed forward at Zed. Zed's hands drew twin silver knives from sheaths inside his boots. He leaped among the men, slitting one's throat in a spray of blood as his other blade sliced off a second man's nose. The noseless man staggered backwards, ichor pouring through the hands clutching his wound and down the front of his vest. The third made a grab for Zed but he ducked under the reaching arms and planted a blade upwards through the underside of the man's chin, sealing his mouth shut and delivering a lethal blow as the blade pierced the brain. Zed let go of the blade, spinning to face the last of the men. Zed stabbed his chest a dozen times in a single second, splashing the walls with the man's insides in a violent display of supernatural speed. The noseless man was on his knees, bleeding and whimpering. Zed walked by him to stand in front of the Alpha.

"You ready to surrender now, Larry?" Zed grinned.

The big man cracked his knuckles and roared at Zed. Muscles grew under his clothing, ripping them, as fur sprouted over his body. His teeth were pushed from his mouth, clattering to the floor, as they were replaced by razor sharp wolf fangs. He sprang at Zed.

Zed jumped to meet him. With superhuman speed, Zed drove the blades of both his knives into the man's throat and flipped over him. He landed on his feet as the big man's corpse skidded on across the floor into a stack of boxes.

There was blood everywhere and Zed could hear the commotion outside the stockroom. It was time to go. He sprinted to the open loading dock and leaped off it onto the pavement outside. He took off like a bolt of lightning, back towards the mountains. His work here was done. The Changed would scatter and he would deal with the rest of them later.

As Zed ran, he thought of Sarah. Perhaps, it was time to pay her a long overdue visit. He'd heard she was pregnant and God knew their pack could use some new blood.

Skyfall

BRIAN FARR WAS ON THE INTERSTATE WHEN IT BEGAN. His day at the office had been a long one. He wanted nothing more than to go home and enjoy a good horror flick on the DV-R. The dropship plummeted from the sky in the distance. Its giant engines wailing like a multitude of Banshees. The ship dove, swooping over the long crowded road ahead of him. The wake of its afterburners tossed cars, vans, and eighteen-wheelers about like they were children's toys swept up in a tornado. Brian watched it all in horror, a white-knuckled grip on his steering wheel. Out of instinct, he slammed on the brakes. Another car slammed into his Toyota from behind, jarring his teeth and sending him bouncing forward in his seat. His seatbelt snapped him back upright as the airbag activated, blocking his view of the death and carnage on the road. Brian flung open his door, leaping from the car, to stare at the massive ship disappearing over the horizon. The ship was jet black and shaped like a diamond.

People were screaming all around him. Crushed and broken vehicles, the dead and dying, and those brave enough to rush forward and try to help the unfortunate souls, filled the entire roadway ahead of Brian. He had seen a lot of things in his fifty years but nothing like this. His knees threatened to give way from the overpowering smells of fear and blood that filled the air. He sat back down in the driver's seat, deflating the airbag violently, and flicked on the radio. Brian leaned over and dug through the glove box for his emergency pack of smokes. He tore the pack open and lit up as the radio scanned through the channels.

"This attack is happening on a global scale! Ships have been sighted over the United States, Europe, China, and Australia!" one frantic newscaster's voice screamed. The radio clicked to another channel. "No one knows where these ships are coming from or how they managed to reach the Earth without being detected!" The channel switched again. "It's clear these aliens are hostile. There are reports of ground troops being deployed at all sites where these ships have touched down." The radio continued to cycle through. "We are at war, folks!" a woman's voice was shouting. "We are at war!"

Brian flipped the radio off. He sat there smoking, too stunned to do anything else, as chaos filled the interstate around him. Half a pack later, the road was clear except for corpses and abandoned vehicles. The sun was sinking in the sky and not a single radio station remained broadcasting as he gave in and checked them once more. From the way the last reports had sounded, the war was already over. Brian ground out his cigarette in the car's ashtray and knew this wasn't a nightmare. It was real and he was alone, still an hour away from home thanks to his long daily commute back and forth from the city, with no idea of what he should he do. He glanced at his cell, wondering if it still worked. There was no signal. Pocketing what remained of his cigarettes and his phone, he got out of the car. All he had wanted was a normal life but he supposed that simply wasn't in the cards. His brothers and sisters were out there somewhere and his crazy old uncle too. Knowing them, they were already busy at what they did best and were kicking some E.T. tail. God help me, Brian thought as he started walking towards home. It was time to join the Family.

* * *

Alarm klaxons blared throughout the *U.S.S. Banner*. Men and women raced for their stations. Among them, Daniel Farr hurried for the deck. He was the chief security officer of the ship and had no intention of letting it fall into the aliens' hands or whatever they had underneath those armored suits they wore. The massive dropship had swept in from the dark clouds above before a single one of the carrier's aircraft could be scrambled. The alien ship had withstood near point blank fire from the *Banner*'s weapons systems without so much a noticeable ding on its black, armored underbelly. It had emitted something akin to a targeted EMP that disabled much the *U.S.S. Banner*'s ability to fight back. As he stepped onto the deck, the first of the alien boarders dropped from the sky. It landed only yards from where he stood with the loud clang of metal striking metal as the heavy boots of its mechanized suit hit the deck. Daniel could hear the whine of servo-motors as it rose upright and turned to face him. The thing was shaped like a man, two arms, two legs, one head, but it smelt altogether unnatural, like an odd mix of rotten eggs and snail slime, discernible even through its armor. The thing was over eight feet tall, its right arm ending in some sort of tribarrel weapon that began to spin and whir to life as it took aim at him. Daniel raised the P-90 he carried and hosed the monster on full auto. Sparks flew as his bullets ricocheted off its black armor. Its spinning tribarrel flashed as a stream of ultra-sonic projectiles shredded his chest, nearly cutting Daniel in half. He flopped to the deck, his body's regenerative abilities straining to hold what was left of him together and heal. From where he lay, Daniel watched a squad of his men try to make a stand against two of the armored monsters. Their submachine guns chattered, spitting shell casings, as their bullets pinged harmless off the black suits without so much as nicking them. One of his men was carrying a grenade launcher. Several of the other died buying him time to get off a shot. The grenade struck the faceplate of the lead monster, detonating on impact. The thing's armored form staggered for a moment before it slumped forward. Yellowish goo oozed through the shattered faceplate, leaving thick trails over the thing's chest, before the thing thudded onto the deck and lay still. The second monster finished his men with a sweep of its tribarrel, painting the deck red with their blood and the mangled pieces of their bodies.

Daniel's wounds had closed. He hauled himself back to his feet. The battle was lost. Over eighteen of the armored things were clomping about the deck and Lord only knew how many more had already made their way below into the bowels of the carrier. For the first time in years, Daniel Farr knew fear, real fear that clawed at his gut. He had to escape, but how? For whatever reason, the aliens seemed to want to take the *Banner* intact.

He ran for the closest of the lifeboats and hoped the aliens would never notice something so small and unthreatening making waves the Hell out of here.

* * *

The streets of Brian's neighborhood were like a war zone. Several houses near his own were burning openly. A crumpled minivan with an F-150 sticking out of its side blacked the main intersection. Thankfully however, there were few bodies along the road. A man lay on his back, rotting, gutted by what must have been a shotgun blast. At the end of his drive, Brian found a woman with a broken spine. The top half of her body was twisted fully around above her legs. Brian guessed she'd been hit by a speeding car or truck during its panicked flight to. . .somewhere. Where could you run when your enemy controlled the sky?

The front door to his house was open as Brian climbed the steps to his porch. Looters? he wondered in the fraction of a second before Zed's scent reached him on the wind. As if on cue, his gray-haired uncle appeared in the doorway.

"Hey, boy! How's the suburb life been treating you?" Zed greeted him with a wide smile. Brian ignored him, pushing his way into the house. He walked to the fridge. The power was out but the temperature inside wasn't quite equal to that of the kitchen's air yet. Brian took a beer and headed back to the living room to sink into his favorite chair. Zed followed him.

"Come on, boy," Zed urged him, "ain't you got nothing to say to your uncle?"

Brian frowned. "Drop the southern bit, Zed. That accent never suited you anyway."

Zed laughed. Brian downed half his beer and stared at the old man. "Why are you here?"

"Just dropped by for a visit. What's it been, five years? Ten? I can't keep track anymore."

"The whole world just got invaded, Zed. Somehow, I don't think this is a social call."

Zed took chair next to Brian's. "That obvious, huh?" Zed plopped his booted feet onto the top of the coffee table and stretched out. "I used to hate it when your uncle Graham would do this to me so I guess I'll get right to it. You may have noticed the humans aren't coping too well with what's happening out there. These. . ." Zed paused as if searching for the right word, "invaders are kicking their tail too, hard and fast, every which way. Well, some of us *others* are getting together a group to do some kicking back. We live here too, ya know? Anyway, the Family is gonna be part of it. I, we, need you, Brian." Zed leaned closer to him. "We wolves stick together."

"I'm not a warrior like mom was, Zed, and I'm certainly not a hero."

"You don't know what you are until you try. Besides, what else are you gonna do? Sit here in the dark, drinking warm beer while the world falls apart around you? You're a Farr, Brian, so I know you're better than that."

"How in the Hades do you even have a plan already?" Brian asked, finishing his beer.

"Your sister, Jennifer, saw this coming two days ago. Everybody but you and Daniel have already joined up and come back. You can bet Daniel will too but we can't locate him at the moment. The navel group his ship was part of was on active duty in the Gulf when the crap hit the fan."

The sound of a helicopter landing in the street outside tore Brian's attention from his uncle.

"That's our ride," Zed grinned. "You coming?"

Brian nodded. "It's not like I have any choice."

* * *

Simon had drawn the short straw. Sometimes he wondered if Brook rigged the whole thing because it seemed like he always did. He cranked up the car's radio, singing along with the words to "Take on Me" with a wicked grin as he jerked the steering wheel one way than the other, dodging the blasts ripping up chunks of the road and the car. The engine whined, his foot keeping the gas pedal pressed to the floorboard. Ahead of him, three armored aliens were making short work of a unit of soldiers trapped inside a burning garage. He hated to call the aliens "mechs" because their suits weren't much larger than a man. Each of them stood only eight feet tall despite the amount of firepower they packed. The term worked for now though so he ran with it. The only mech that bothered to pay attention to his approach was one Hell of a lousy shot. Either that or it knew nothing about cars. His vehicle took several bursts from the mech's tribarrel arm that sliced through it as if it were paper and blew out the forward windshield. Thankfully, none of them hit the engine block.

"Yeah!" Simon shouted as he plowed into the thing at over a hundred miles per hour. The car folded up with the grinding sound of compacting metal and the mech was swept under its crumbling wreckage. Simon jumped from the mess just as the whole thing exploded in a blossoming could of flames and shrapnel. He hit the pavement rolling. The other two mechs noticed him now. Both of their gun hands swept towards him, high velocity rounds cutting holes in the road as their streams of fire closed in on him.

"A little help, guys!" he yelled into his comm headset as he scrambled to his feet and started running. Glancing over his shoulder, he saw Mordred step from the shadows of a nearby alleyway behind the mechs. His brother's hands weaved through the air as his lips moved, speaking a tongue long lost to the world of modern man. The ground beneath the mechs became black and soft like tar. They fell into it as if they had been standing on the top of a frozen lake and the ice under their feet had suddenly given way. The ground instantly became solid again. Of the two mechs, all that remained of one was a hand sticking up through the concrete of the road; the other was buried up to its chest. It took aim at Mordred and opened up with its tribarrel blazing. Mordred was gone though, vanished into the darkness once more. Simon stopped running as Brook came sprinting toward the trapped alien, twin, twirling blades in her hands. The poor creature lost its tribarrel to her first swing, its gun hand clanging as it bounced along the road. Brook plunged her second blade into and through the thing's armored head. Sallow blood leaked from the holes she made as Brook jerked her sword free of the armor. Brook was wiping her blade clean with a piece of cloth from her pocket as Simon walked back toward the scene.

"It's okay!" he called to the soldiers in the garage, "you can come out now!"

Five ash-covered, coughing infantry men stumbled into the street. One of them looked at Brook, his eyes moving over the well-proportioned curves of her body, then to her sword. "Who in the Hell are you people?" he asked.

Simon laughed, slapping the soldier on his back. "We're special forces, mate, *real* special forces."

* * *

As the helicopter flew over Charlotte, Brian stared at the raging fires below and wondered how the aliens had done so much damage so quickly. As if reading his mind, Zed said, "Those armored freaks ain't lacking for firepower, boy. One of their suits is worth about three of our tanks. Tough sons of guns to kill too. Standard armor-piercing rounds don't do jack to them unless you hit a faceplate or a joint in the armor." Zed tapped his headset. "I'm getting constant intel updates from Eyes. She's monitoring everything happening out there that she can. The army ain't out of the fight yet even if it does kind of look that way."

"Where are we headed?" Brian asked.

"Got ourselves a base of sorts up in the mountains. Eyes and Jennifer are there coordinating the others. Simon, Mordred, Brook, and Kyle are in the field with Grunt and his boys. They're trying to round up and salvage what forces they can."

Brian didn't recognize some of the names Zed was spouting at him. "Whoa. Slow down. Who in the heck are Eyes and these others you mentioned?"

Zed gave him a sad look. "For a lot of years, I worked for the church, hunting down any of the Changed that chose to prey on the humans, but when your mother died, I guess I kind of sold out, joined up with the C.I.A. Been running black ops ever since. I may be pushing two hundred and ten but I can't bring myself to retire. *That* would kill me faster than any silver bullet ever could." Zed paused as the copter started to descend. He barked something at the pilot and then turned back to Brian. "Anyway, we wolves aren't the only misfits out there. Eyes and Kyle were assigned to me as my support."

Brian raised an eyebrow at his uncle.

"They're good folk even if they are a touch off."

Several soldiers rushed to meet them as he and Zed exited the copter, stepping onto the lawn of an ancient looking mansion. Brian saw many of its upper windows sported gun emplacements. Numerous other helicopters, trucks, and even a tank surrounded the place.

"It ain't N.O.R.A.D. but it'll do for us," Zed yelled at him over the noise of the slowing helicopter blades as the soldiers reached them.

"Colonel Farr!" one them shouted. "You're needed inside, sir!"

"Colonel?" Brian mouthed the word at Zed.

"Like I said, boy, I sold out."

Oh God help us, Brian thought as the soldiers escorted them into the mansion.

* * *

The mansion's huge dining hall had been converted into a war room. Monitors covered the walls, displaying various locations from around the globe and newscasts that were still on the air. There were several communications stations set up as well. Men and women in uniform rushed about doing only Lord knew what. All this was beyond Brian. He had never really been an adventurer like rest of his family. It had been one of the sore spots between himself and his mother, Sarah. She had respected his choices in life but he had always felt that despite his success in the world of entertainment, she had been disappointed in how he turned out. He hadn't been there at her side when old age finally claimed her shortly after her one hundred and ninety-sixth birthday. Her body had simply given out. By all rights, Zed should have been dead too, but somehow his hyper metabolism that gave him his speed also increased his natural regeneration. A human would easily mistake him as a healthy sixty year old with a spry step.

"Eyes!" Zed yelled into the sea of chaos. "These boys tell me you need me" A head perked up in the crowd. From a distance, she appeared a very attractive blonde with a slender and tight figure but as she turned to the sound of Zed's voice, Brian felt his jaw drop. Two bulbous orbs, twice the size of his fists, protruded from her face above her nose and mouth. Each was a mass of clustered-together eyeballs, much like a spider's.

"Colonel," she said in a frustrated voice, "we've lost communications with the Ninth."

Zed cursed, smashing a fist into the comm station she stood in front of. "They were the last active unit in Georgia, weren't they?"

"I'm afraid so, sir."

Zed noticed Brian. "Don't stare, son. It ain't polite.".

"Eyes, this is my nephew I was telling you about, Brian. You'll have to forgive him. He doesn't get out much."

Eyes nodded at Brian as he managed to get out a strained, "Hello."

"Wait until you meet Kyle," Zed teased him.

* * *

Kyle clung to the roof of the tunnel. Two of the mechs were stupid enough to follow him inside. The footsteps of their heavy metal feet echoed off the tunnel's walls among the sea of abandoned cars. Kyle didn't need to breathe. He remained completely silent and motionless, waiting for the aliens to get closer. Night had fallen outside the tunnel and the city's power was offline. The darkness was total and complete but Kyle's red eyes could see the mechs; he watched their approach as clearly as if it were a bright sunny day. He had no fear of their weapons. For all their technology, the aliens, like Earth soldiers, relied upon metal projectiles as their primary means of attack. Kyle let go of the ceiling, his patience giving out, as his flesh dissolved into vapor. He could hear the two mechs chattering back and forth in a series of clicks and hisses, no doubt about the fog that now filled the air around them. One of the things panicked. It opened up with its tribarrel, hosing a row of nearby cars and the tunnel's wall. Sparks and shards of concrete and glass flew. The other mech issued a series of frantic popping noises. Lowering its still-smoking gun hand, the mech that had panicked scanned the tunnel still searching for him as Kyle coalesced into a solid form between the two of them. He grabbed the smoking tribarrel hand of the closest mech and crushed it under the pressure of his grip as he shoved the other mech away. His push sent its heavy armored form flying into the hood of a Chevy truck. The truck's hood folded inward under the mech's weight before the alien rolled off to bounce onto the tunnel's floor. The mech with the crippled tribarrel took a swing at him but Kyle dodged under its arm. He came up with a double-fisted blow that shattered its faceplate. The thing inside the armor squealed. Green eyes glowed in the darkness from within the armor before Kyle rammed a fist into the thing's face, reducing it to pulp. Yellow goo splashed outward. He yanked his arm free of the dying alien's twitching form as he heard the remaining mech's tribarrel whir to life. The bullets streaked harmlessly through him as he shifted into a cloud of vapor once more. Kyle reformed behind the armored alien. His arms closed about it in a bear hug. The metal of the armor whined as it was crushed tighter and tighter into the alien inside of it. When he was sure the alien was dead, he dropped the twisted armor, letting it clatter to the tunnel floor at his feet. His trap had worked perfectly, but what did slaying two of the mechs matter when there were thousands more in the United States alone? With a shrug, his flesh melted, his bones reshaping, as he became a giant bat-like creature. His newly formed leathery wings flapping, Kyle flew out of the tunnel into the night beyond.

* * *

Daniel sat helplessly in the small lifeboat, staring at its motor. He'd exhausted its fuel an hour before. In his flight from the *U.S.S. Banner*, he'd lost track of his bearings and was now adrift with little hope of rescue. He knew how to read the stars, but during the day the ocean and sky were the same in all directions. His radio had been blown to bits when the mech had shot him on the deck. He possessed nothing but his sidearm and a stubborn determination to get home. His kind couldn't die from dehydration or starvation. At worst, his body would simply shut down, going into a dormant state until someone or something revived him. Of course, that didn't mean it wouldn't be painful or that he wouldn't go insane before it happened. He knew Zed would be searching for him. His crazy, old uncle was likely organizing some kind of resistance against the invaders right now, and that meant he'd want all of the Family at his side.

Maybe he should have listened to Zed and stayed on with his uncle's black op team instead of seeking his own destiny in the Navy. Daniel had just wanted to find his own path in life and figured he had enough blood on his hands already from his younger days spent with his mom and uncle before she had died. The Navy had been his escape from the questionable morality of his uncle's missions, a place where he could make a difference without Zed always looking over his shoulder. He loved Zed. He really did, but he had too much of his mom's sense of discipline in him to ever fully see eye to eye with him. His uncle was as reckless and wild as they came despite his age. How the United States government could risk giving Zed all the leeway and authority he had with his team, Daniel would never understand.

With a sigh, he gave up trying to get the motor going again and settled in, stretching out in the boat to gaze up at the clouds above. If he was really, really lucky, maybe Mordred would come for him. Mordred had inherited his Uncle Samuel's aptitude for magic, or so Zed claimed. Daniel didn't believe in magic, at least not the kind Zed meant, but there was no denying that Mordred could bend reality itself to his will somehow. Mordred was far from all-powerful. His abilities—or spells he called them—had their limits.

Daniel closed his eyes and decided to do the only thing he could do until help came. . . Wait.

* * *

Brian sat in the makeshift briefing room with Jennifer, waiting on the others to show up.

"I know you don't want to be here," Jennifer said, breaking the silence, "but it's good to see you again, Brian."

"What's it like?" he asked. "I mean working with Zed? This life of trying to keep the world safe?"

Jennifer laughed. "I don't get out much, Brian. It's not like I'm out there on the frontlines with the rest of them. . . Besides, I never had a shot at a normal life like you did. Everything's pretty much boring when you see it before it happens."

"Did you. . ?"

Jennifer nodded sadly. "Yeah, I saw Mom's death coming but sometimes there are things you can't change no matter how much you want to or might try."

Brian saw the pain in his sister's eyes and wished he hadn't asked *that* question. He put his hands on the table top and changed the subject. "Mordred still a creep?"

"He's a jerk. Some things never change."

"Why, sister, that's not a nice thing to say," a cold voice called from the corner of the room. Mordred, Brook, and Simon stepped through one the mage's shadow gates. The darkness rippled behind them as it closed. Brian watched as Brook's eyes went wide as she saw him sitting at the table. Simon came running over as he yelled, "Brian!"

Brian stood up to meet Simon, who barreled into him. He gently broke free of Simon's embrace.

"Hello, Brian," Mordred said.

He nodded at Mordred. As usual, the mage was dressed in solid black and the cowl of his long cloak obscured the features of his face, masking them in shadow.

"Don't tell me Zed drafted you," Brook said with a smile as she moved forward and offered him her hand.

Brian took it, clutching it tightly. "You could call it that," Brian shrugged. "This certainly wasn't my idea."

"Yee-haw!" Simon yelled. "It's about time too! You have no idea the kind of fun you've been missing, bro."

Zed walked in with a pale, grim-faced man Brian didn't recognize.

"Mordred, why are you still here?" Zed snapped.

Mordred glared at the gray-haired speedster but said nothing. He turned back to Brian with a half bow of farewell then blinked out of existence.

Zed grunted. "He should be back with Daniel soon. In the meantime, we got ourselves a war to plan so let's get to it."

Brian saw Zed glance around the room. "Where in the Hades is Grunt?"

Brian noticed none of the others seemed to have any idea who Zed was talking about either. Eyes appeared in the room's doorway. "He's in the field, sir."

"I thought I recalled everyone for this meeting," Zed grumbled.

"You did, sir," Eyes reminded him. "I will not repeat what his response was when I relayed your order."

A low growl arose in Zed's throat.

* * *

A group of seven mechs marched towards the F.B.I. headquarters, one in the lead, the others behind it in a tight formation. Two more mechs awaited the column on the buildings steps. The street was littered with the bodies of agents, S.W.A.T. team members, and scattered soldiers. Grunt watched from behind the cover of an overturned armored truck. He and his boys had arrived too late to prevent the bloodshed but they were here now and those alien scumbags were going to pay. He tapped the side of the comm unit on his ear. "Marcus, everybody in position?"

"You know it, boss," Marcus's voice answered.

Grunt really hated it when Marcus called him that. He might be the current Alpha of the Changed but he still didn't like it. Alan Barth was his given name and he was a simple man, born for violence and with muscles to spare, thus his nickname. A lot of folks would have found being called Grunt belittling, but not him. He thought it fit perfectly. Before he'd ascended to be Alpha, through no choice of his own, Grunt had been the main enforcer of his people, traveling the globe and making problems disappear. Now he was leading them in an unexpected war in which the chances of their survival were bleak. As yet, the aliens were occupied with the humans, but when there were no humans left, he could bet they would turn their attention to the Changed and learn of his people's weakness to sliver. The invaders already knew that fire worked against them, but it took them time to realize who they were fighting and switch tactics in any given engagement. That edge had kept the bulk of his boys alive so far. His race was small in number and all their warriors were with him, the rest of his people still blending in among the humans and seeking refuge where they could.

Grunt checked his AA-12. The heavy shotgun was loaded with the best ammo-piercing rounds money could buy. He tapped his comm unit again. "Let's take these armored mothers down!"

As he leaped to his feet and left his cover to get a shot at the mechs, all Hell broke loose around him. Five RPGs streaked towards the column of mechs from nearby alleyways and rooftops where his boys were positioned. Two of the mechs launched countermeasures, stopping all but one of them from reaching its target. It slammed into the rear-most mech and exploded in a ball of orange flame. Grunt fired off shot after shot with his AA-12. His first one blew a hole in a mech's leg, splashing the street with yellow goo. The mech dropped to one knee. He caved in another's faceplate with a trio of rounds as the others returned fire. A mass of shrieking micro-missiles flew from four of the mechs' shoulders, targeting the squads who'd launched the RPGs. Simultaneously, two of the mechs spun toward Grunt himself, their tribarrels blazing. He dove behind an abandoned patrol car that sat in the street between him and the mechs' position, but the aliens' bullets tore through it like it was rotted vegetation. Several of the rounds ripped through his back as well, erupting from his chest and leaving gaping exit wounds in their wake. Grunt snarled the pain away as Bruce and Tucker, two of his boys, hit the mechs from the other side of the street. Their own AA-12s sent two more mechs clattering to the pavement, leaking yellow, to lay still. The mech in command caught on quick to what was happening, issuing a series of pops and clicks at his troops. As Bruce and Tucker closed in on the things, they were met with combined blasts from three of the mechs' secondary flame weapons. Grunt head them screaming but couldn't see through the fire that engulfed the entire area of the street where they had been.

"No!" Grunt howled, jumping over what remained of the patrol car and cracking open the head of a mech with a lucky shot. It stumbled into one of its brethren beside it as it went down, saving Grunt from a stream of fire that surely would have come his way but instead blazed upwards into the sky.

Marcus' voice came over his headset. "There's two more columns on their way, boss. We need to bug out now!"

Grunt dodged a fresh wave of fire aimed at him, sprinting for the closet alley. "Do it!" he ordered. "Fall back! We'll meet up at the extraction point!"

He reached the alley as yet another burst of flame singed the hair on his back and kept right on running.

* * *

"Wait a minute," Brook said to Zed, "You don't mean. . .?"

Brian watched as Zed nodded.

"Yep, that Grunt."

"Oh that's just great," Brook threw up her hands in an expression of hurt and rage.

Brian had no idea who they were talking about.

"Uncle," Simon shook his head, "I may be a touch crazy but even I wouldn't have gone that far."

"Who is this Grunt?" Brian spoke up. "I mean what's the big deal?"

Brook's eyes flashed yellow with rage but then she seemed to remember how out of touch he was with the world the rest of them lived and fought in. "Brian," she said in a voice that was straining to stay calm, "Grunt is the main enforcer of the Changed. If our current intel is correct, he may even be their Alpha now."

"He is," Zed admitted. "Look, trust me, I realize how long the Purebloods and Changed have been at war better than any of you but those alien freaks want us all dead. Even with Kyle here at our side, there's only seven of us total that can take this fight to them. Grunt has at least forty warriors, if not more, assuming he and his boys haven't been slaughtered out there yet. We need their muscle."

"One Pureblood is worth ten of the Changed," Brook reminded Zed.

"Yeah well, have you looked at how many mechs have already landed?" Zed took a step closer to Brook. "None of us are truly immortal, not even Kyle. A temporary alliance with the Changed is the only hope we have of even hurting those freaks in armor enough to matter."

"I don't like it," Simon turned to Brook. "But he's right and you know it."

Brian had never met one of the Changed but he knew well what they were. They were wolves like his family, but not real ones born to what they were. The Changed were humans who'd been attacked either by a Pureblood or one of the Changed who'd managed to survive with only a scrape or a bite. The wound transferred the essence of the wolf to them, altering their DNA close to that of a Pureblood's.

At the first full moon or moment of experiencing strong anger, they became a wolf themselves, driven by instinct and primal urges, usually with no one to help them understand what they had become. Since the beginning of both species, the Purebloods had killed the Changed on sight not only to protect humanity but also to protect the secret of their existence. In the last century however, the Changed had grown more organized. It was rare that a member of the Changed didn't get help soon after their first transformation. The Farr family was the only surviving line of Purebloods, and as thus, the war between the Purebloods and the Changed had mostly ceased except for minor skirmishes in places where rogue members of the Changed reverted to the old ways and made humankind their prey. Neither side liked or trusted the other even today and most encounters between the two usually led to bloodshed as thousands upon thousands of years of hatred was not so easily let go of. Brian's mother, Sarah, often told him stories of the Changed and the war. Even he knew Zed was taking a large gamble by inviting the Changed to stand with them.

"This Grunt is already proving the Changed can't be trusted, uncle," Brook argued, "or he would be here wouldn't he?" Zed frowned but said nothing more about the Changed, instead gesturing at Eyes. She flipped a switch on the high tech gauntlet covering her left arm from wrist to elbow and a holographic display of the United States sprang to life in the center of the table. Red dots speckled the map, moving slowly across it; a single blue orb covered the city of New York.

"Those red dots represent drop ships and divisions of mechs," Zed told them all.

"What's the big blue one?" Brian asked.

"It appears our enemy is building some sort of massive structure in New York. Our best guess is that it is some sort of terra-forming device. We believe that once it's fully operational, those buggers plan to use it to make our world like the one they come from. If it's activated, that'll be the end, folks. Humanity and the Earth as we know it will be gone." Zed leaned onto the table, his palms flat against its surface. "It's also where we have to hit them."

"But if we destroy that thing they're building, what's to stop them from just building another one?" Simon asked.

Zed smiled. "New York has also become their primary stronghold on Earth. After we blow that heap of metal to bits. . ."

"We're going to steal a ship," Brook finished for him.

"Exactly," Zed laughed. "And we're going up to that mothership of theirs and make them pay. We destroy it and everything gets easier down here. The war on the surface will become nothing more than a mop-up operation as the mechs' run out of supplies and ammo with nowhere to turn for help."

"That's just crazy enough to work," Simon was on his feet. "I'm so in. When do we leave?"

* * *

Daniel watched his shadow grow, becoming a mass of swirling darkness that engulfed the small lifeboat he was adrift in. The blazing heat of the sun vanished, replaced by a creeping cold that reached his bones. "Mordred?" Daniel asked the darkness.

A deeper pool of black in its center coalesced into the form of his brother. "I am here," Mordred answered him. "But we must not tarry. Even as we speak, Zed and the others are laying plans of retribution for what has been done to our world."

"I figured as much," Daniel grunted.

The darkness gave way to the artificial lights on the ceiling of the old mansion Zed had claimed for the group's headquarters. Daniel's legs wobble adjusting to the lack of waves rolling beneath his feet. He glared at Mordred. "I hate it when you do that."

"This way," Mordred said, and led him down the hall towards the makeshift briefing room. The others were emerging from it, their meeting over. Daniel did a double take as he spotted Brian walking out with Zed and Jennifer.

"Brian?" he shouted. "Is that really you?"

A sad smile played over Brian's face. "Guess I'm one of the team now from the looks of things."

Daniel chuckled. "I haven't seen you since. . ." He stopped himself. The last time they had been together was at their mother's funeral.

Mordred stepped forward. "Are you sure this is what you want, Brian? Give the word and I can take you home."

"Leave him be, Mordred," Zed warned the mage. "We need him."

Mordred frowned. "When was the last time you even used your gift, Brian? For that matter, how long has it been since you even became a wolf?"

Before Brian could answer, Daniel moved between him and Mordred. "He'll be fine. Won't you, Brian?"

Brian didn't answer.

"Everybody get geared up. We leave in fifteen," Zed told them, and followed Eyes towards the war room.

"What's wrong with him?" Mordred asked.

"Trouble with the Changed he recruited," Brian said. "Their leader, Grunt, is already disobeying his orders."

Mordred snorted. "What did he expect?"

"This is where I say goodbye," Jennifer spoke up, placing a hand on Brian's shoulder. "Daniel, you look after him okay?"

Daniel nodded. "You know I will."

* * *

The strike team consisted of Kyle, Daniel, Book, Mordred, Simon, Zed, and Brian. Zed was still off with Eyes as Brian followed the others into a room filled with weapons and armor. Mordred and Kyle waited near the room's door. It seemed neither of them needed to "gear up". Simon slung an automatic shotgun over his shoulder by its strap and picked up something that looked like a grenade launcher. Brian stood beside him, overwhelmed by the choice of weapons.

"Don't be stingy, bro," Simon urged him. "Grab whatever you want or think you'll need."

"I don't know where to start," Brian said in complete honesty.

"He's a total newbie," Brook reminded Simon. "Here," she said, passing Brian a sword like the two she wore in scabbards on her back. "It's enchanted like mine so it'll do the job and you don't need to worry about reloading it."

Brian accepted the sword and hefted it, getting a feel for its balance and weight. He'd always loved blades, and while he wasn't anywhere near as skilled as Brook, he supposed it was the best choice. "Thank you," he said.

Simon gave him a disapproving look. "Guns are more fun, man. They make a lot more noise."

Brian ignored Simon and turned to Kyle. "Are you really. . .?"

"A vampire?" Kyle asked. "Yes, I am. Does that bother you, little wolf?"

"Hey!" Daniel warned. "Lay off him."

Kyle raised a hand in gesture of peace. "I meant no insult."

"It's okay," Brian said. "Do you mind if I ask how old you are?"

"Old enough to have seen Rome fall."

"Are there others like you?"

"Once, yes. . . But no longer."

"He's the last of his kind just like we're the last of the Purebloods left in this world," Zed said, stepping into the room. "Glad to have him around, though. It's nice not to be the oldest one around here anymore."

Zed poked Kyle with his elbow but the vampire didn't respond to his jab. Kyle's expression remained cold and aloof.

"If everyone is ready, shall I take us to New York, uncle?" Mordred asked.

"Not yet." Zed drew his twin revolvers and checked their chambers with a flip of his wrists, popping them open and closed in a single fluid movement.. "We got one other stop to make first." Zed grinned at Brian. "Take us to Grunt, Mordred. That kid's got some explaining to do."

* * *

Grunt reached the extraction point hoping to see his boys piling onto a group of Blackhawks but the helicopters were nowhere to be seen. Only Marcus, his second in command, and fifteen of his boys were there. He could see from Marcus's eyes that no more would be coming..

"It wasn't easy getting out of the city, boss," Marcus said. "We figure we're all that's left."

"And the copters?"

"Can't raise them on the comm." Marcus confirmed his suspicions and then asked, "You think those snotty Purebloods set us up?"

"Doubt it." Grunt studied the treeline and the farmhouse they had gathered at. Five miles down the road was a city, but where they were now seemed like the middle of nowhere. That's North Carolina for you, he thought. "What about the Mechs? Any sign of them?"

"You can bet they're coming, boss. Based on the reports of the others here, who weren't in my group as we fell back, there were at least three columns tasked with trying to stop our retreat."

"Great. Just great," Grunt snarled.

"Should we dig in or try to run?" Marcus stared at him, waiting for an answer.

Grunt weighed their options. Most likely, the Mechs had shot the Blackhawks out of the sky while they were still inbound. As crazy as that old wolf Zed came across, it didn't seem like his style to just abandon them here. The question was, if they stayed would Zed get more help to them in time? They couldn't' survive on much less prolonged engagement with the Mechs. . .but if they ran, they would be on their own for sure.

"Find some cover and let's pray those Pureblood bastards get here before the mechs do."

Marcus started barking orders at the others as Grunt felt a change in the air around them. The temperature dropped by several degrees, the shadows inside the farm's barn grew darker. Grew to a small black thunderhead.

"Zed!" Grunt shouted in relief as the old wolf stepped from the swirling cloud of black inside the barn. The pale man who stunk of death and rot, along with two of Zed's pack, followed him out. Grunt counted three more of the Purebloods inside the barn, including Zed's spell weaver. All of them were ready for battle except for the brown-haired one with glasses who seemed terribly out of place among the rest, despite the sword sheathed on his back.

"I was beginning to think you had left us to die, old man." Grunt made sure his words carried the edge of a veiled threat. He saw Zed take a look at what remained of his bloodied and tired warriors.

"Looks like you boys have seen more than your fair share of dying today already." Zed shook his head. "I thought you were clear as to who was heading up this resistance effort of ours, Grunt. I ordered you to pull out, not go in guns blazing to save a building that was already lost."

"I saw a chance to make a stand and I took it," Grunt said.

"You paid the price for it too."

Grunt felt his cheeks grow hot with anger, but the old man was right, damn him.

The eyes of his boys were on him as Grunt faced the old Pureblood. Grunt didn't dare show weakness or admit failure. He was saved from the awkward moment by the sound of tribarrel fire. A column of seven mechs burst from the trees, closing in on their position. His men were returning fire and preparing to meet them.

"No!" Zed shouted over the cacophony of gunfire. "Get your men into the barn. Mordred will teleport us all out of here."

Grunt hesitated, torn between honor and wisdom.

"We're taking this to *them!*" Zed pointed at the sky. "You with us or not?"

"To the barn!" Grunt screamed at his men. "Fall back!"

Even as he gave the order, Grunt knew it was too late. His hesitation was going to cost lives. Two of his men died howling as waves of flames washed over their flesh, melting it from their bones. A third chose not to listen to him, disregarding the order, transforming as he charged the closest of the mechs. The man's skin tore and split as his bones reshaped and he grew taller. His hybrid form, half wolf, half man, slammed into the mech, taking it to the dirt. His massive fists bashing into the mech's faceplate over and over until it cracked, giving way to his supernatural strength and fury. Grunt didn't stick around to watch him die as more of the mechs closed in, but he heard the whoosh of their flamethrowers and the agonized cries that followed. Grunt dove into the darkness of the barn and then, through magic, the world around him changed. He and his surviving men were atop a skyscraper in what could only be New York City, with Zed and his pack among them. Smoke clogged the air and the city below resembled a scene from a war film. Smaller version of the large alien dropships zipped through the sky and in the distance stood the end of the world. It was a mountain of metal that shimmered with pulses of crackling energy and seemed almost alive. The structure dwarfed the building they stood on towering above the skyline of the city like a great abomination of death and evil.

"There it is," Zed pointed at the thing. "Now we just have to get inside it."

Grunt got himself together and asked the obvious question: "Why didn't your mage just take us there?"

"I can't," Mordred pulled his dark cloak tighter about him. "Something about the energy it's producing blocks my ability to get inside."

"We sure as Hell can't fight our way in," Grunt admitted. "This whole city is swarming with mechs and you can bet they'd all come running if we made a move on the front door."

"Don't worry," Zed assured him, "I have a plan."

"Really?" Grunt mocked the old wolf.

"Seems our alien friends aren't killing every human they come across. According to Eyes, who has been using some of the United States' surviving spy satellites to observe this area, they've been rounding up packs of survivors and taking them into the structure. If we can get a few of us in that way, the rest of us can make enough noise out here for them take advantage of the chaos and blow that thing sky high." Zed motioned to Mordred, who opened his cloak. Hanging impossibly on each side it were two high tech contraptions that looked like bombs.

"What are those?"

Mordred closed his cloak as Zed answered. "Ten mega tons of nuclear boom, mates. We get them in and they'll do the job. I'd rather lose New York City than the world. Anyway, whoever gets in just has to create a hole in the structure's energy field for Mordred to go through, then we'll be on to phase two of the plan."

"So who's going to get captured?" Grunt asked.

* * *

An hour later, Simon, Grunt, and Kyle strolled down a deserted street littered with abandoned cars, smoking rumble, and the occasional bullet-ridden corpse, mangled by fire from an alien tribarrel.

"I swear Brook rigs things so that I am always the one who goes in first," Simon complained. If I didn't know better, I'd think she was trying to get me killed."

"Perhaps she is," Kyle said in a cold, matter-of-fact tone.

"I'm not used to being bait," Grunt snarled.

"Yeah," Simon agreed. "Leaving our weapons with the others really sucked. So who has the bomb we're supposed to blow a hole in this thing with anyway?"

"I do." Kyle patted his stomach. "I ingested it before we left."

Simon was disgusted. "Dude, that's just wrong on so many levels."

Grunt stopped, holding up a hand for the others to do the same. He sniffed the air. "They're here."

"Let us hope they cannot distinguish us from the humans," Kyle whispered as a trio of mechs rounded the corner ahead of them, blocking their path. Grunt threw up his arms, approaching the metal monsters. "Please don't hurt us! We surrender!"

One of the mechs raised its tribarrel at Grunt but instead of the weapon's normal spray of bullets, it spat three darts into the huge man's chest. "Crap," Simon heard Grunt say as he turned back towards them. "These things really work." With that, Grunt toppled face-first onto the pavement.

Simon decided to add some realism so the mechs wouldn't get suspicious about three humans walking up to them and turning themselves over. "Run!" he screamed at Kyle, then spun about, his legs pumping beneath him as he sprinted for the doorway of the closest building. He glanced over his shoulder to see Kyle pick up a metal piece of debris from the street and charge the mechs. Kyle barely made it a few feet towards them before a trio of darts struck him down. Simon reached the building's doorway as a set of darts embedded themselves in the wood of the apartment building's door next to him. He ripped open the door as he heard the popping noise of more darts being fired. Pain stung his back and the world spun before his eyes. Wow. They really do work, he thought before he lost consciousness.

* * *

Simon awoke to Kyle kicking him. The vampire stood above him as he opened his eyes. "Where. .?"

"We're inside the structure, wolf, but we don't have much time," Kyle told him, helping him to his feet.

Simon looked around. They were in what appeared to be a holding cell and they weren't alone. Twenty or so humans shared it with them. The walls of the cell were vastly different than the sleek black metal of the structure's exterior. Simon touched the wall. It felt like it was moving ever so slightly as if it were breathing. When he removed his hand, it came away wet, covered in a slime like substance that had the consistency of jelly. "Eww," he said, shaking the substance off of him.

Grunt walked over to join them where he and Kyle stood. "Glad you finally decided to wake up."

Grunt nervously shot a glance at the cell's door. It was a disturbing, yellowish color and wasn't really a door at all by Earth standards. It was some kind of phlegm membrane that would be better in the body of a person with a sore throat than a high tech terraforming device from another world. "The guards will be back soon," Grunt warned. "You think this room is messed up, wait until you see what the aliens look like without armor."

"They have been taking small groups of humans away every hour or so. Sometimes only two, other times up to five or more. None of the humans have returned," Kyle said as Simon dug a knife out from inside the lining of his boot.

"They sure didn't search us well."

"No. They did not," Kyle agreed, "but they will soon. Each human who has been removed has also been stripped."

"It's wild, man," Grunt cut in, "They wave this weird Star Trek gadget thingy up and down over the ones they take. Whatever it is, the beam of light that comes out of it just eats away everything on that person that isn't a part of them." "I believe it does much more than that," Kyle added, "I think it also makes sure the person scanned is indeed a true human."

"Uh-Oh," Simon frowned. "So we're in trouble then?"

"Big time," Grunt gestured at the knife Simon held, "You might as well toss that thing. It isn't going to do anything but make sure you're one of the next to be taken."

"You sure? That door. . .membrane thing doesn't look that thick."

"Forget it," Grunt shook his head. "Vamp man here snuck close to it an hour ago and tried to push through it. That thing's tougher than steel."

"Oh crap!" one of the humans shouted. "They're coming back!"

* * *

Zed's plan was two-fold. One group would go to war with the mechs a couple of miles from the aliens' terraforming structure in hopes of luring a good portion of its defenders away. The second group would get as close to the thing as possible and strike when the first group had done its job. The first group consisted of Brian, Brook, Daniel, and the remainder of Grunt's boys. The second would be Zed himself along with Mordred and fifty human troops shadow-ported in from the Family's base of operations at the mansion.

Brian was nervous as he, Brook, Daniel, and Marcus, who was Grunt's second in command of the Changed, set up an ambush for a mech patrol. These first few moments of the battle would be the most crucial. They had to hit the mechs hard enough to keep them off balance but not wipe them out entirely. They needed the mechs to call for backup or their efforts would be pointless. Marcus had RPG teams set up on the third floors of two buildings above where the group would make its stand. The rest of the Changed would be waiting in wolf hybrid form to go tooth and nail against the mechs as soon as the shooting started. Brian figured Zed was apparently counting on his ability to keep them in the fight long enough to matter. Brian couldn't remember the last time he'd used his gift. Zed was risking a lot by taking such a chance on him. Whether he wanted to admit it or not, he could stand toe to toe with Mordred and he dwarfed the rest of the Family in terms of sheer power. Perhaps that's why he had never wanted any part of it. He had no choice but to try to use it now though. Brian just hoped he could control it.

"You ready?" Brook asked.

"As I'll ever be," Brian said, crouching behind the cover of an overturned eighteen wheeler with her and Marcus.

"Good. We've got incoming," Marcus told them. "Seven mechs heading straight down the street towards us just like we planned it. Give the word and I'll have the boys light 'em up." Brook drew her swords, giving each a single spin as she readied them. "Do it!" She snarled.

Marcus gave the signal over the comm. Brian peaked around the end of the truck as RPGs streaked towards the column of mechs. The armored aliens were taken completely off guard by the attack here in the center of their stronghold of power on Earth. One mech took an RPG to its chest, its armor cracking open and spilling out the pulped remains of the alien inside. The second RPG detonated between two others, doing damage to both and knocking them from their feet. A chorus of howls arose all around the column as the confused and panicked mechs drew their ranks closer together and hosed the nearby buildings with their tribarrels. A rain of shattering glass from blown-out windows fell over them, clattering harmlessly off their armored forms. Then, as one, seven wolf creatures came tearing at them. The mechs flattened as the wolves crashed into them. Claws slashed at and sparked against alien metal. Snarls of rage intermingled with the roar of gunfire.

"Two more columns coming in!" Marcus shouted. One marched up the street straight towards their position from behind. The other moved in to assist the already engaged original column and added their firepower against the wolves.

"Brian," Brook said, grabbing him by the arm, "this is it. Marcus and I can help Grunt's boys but you're going to have to handle the third column with your gift."

Brian stared into Brook's eyes, seeing the desperation there.

"You won't be alone," Daniel told him, raising his AA-12. "I got your back."

Brian nodded slowly. "I'll try."

Brook and Marcus darted for the battle up the street. Brook issued a blood curdling battle cry as she leaped through the air at a mech. Her blades taking both of its arms off before she knocked it into the midst of the second column. Marcus's shotgun thundered repeatedly in rapid succession, armor-piercing slugs staggering one of the mechs before another shot blew its faceplate to pieces.

"Come on!" Daniel jerked Brian to his feet as the third column of mechs came to a halt and tribarrels rose in their direction. Brian reached deep within himself, awakening his gift after years of slumber. His eyes exploded with blue light like mini-supernovas. Power flowed through his veins, his very soul. He felt alive, invulnerable, and most of all angry. The seven mechs of the third column opened fire. Brian raised a hand at the bullets as they flew toward him. A barrier of shimmering, translucent energy caught the bullets and threw them back at the mechs. The four closest mechs were shredded by their own rounds, bullets ripping into and through their armor, spraying yellow blood over their comrades behind them. One of the remaining mechs turned to run as the flamethrower units of the other two flared to life. However, they never had a chance to use them. Brian stepped forward, clenching each of his hands into fists. The two mechs were crushed like empty soda cans where they stood. As their twisted forms thudded to the pavement, Brian heard Daniel whisper, "Damn." Brian sank to one knee, momentarily winded.

Brook danced among the mechs of the second column. The sword in her right hand took one's head as her left cut a trail of parted metal and yellow blood across another's chest. She spun to finish the mech she had wounded, both blades gutting it in a combined swipe upwards through its stomach. Marcus ran up beside her, taking aim at a mech she hadn't noticed while she dealt with the two she had just sent to Hell. Its flamethrower weapon was pointed at her as Marcus emptied his AA-12's drum into the mech's chest.

Almost all of the wolves were dead. Their corpses lay burning on the pavement and the smell of cooking flesh and hair made her gray. Marcus screamed as a wave of fire washed his back, setting his clothes aflame. Brook shoved him from her path as he howled in pain, burnt skin sloughing off his back and face. She charged the mech that had issued his death sentence as it fired again. The powerful muscles of her legs sent her flying over the wave of fire to land directly in front of it. It caught her swinging first as her blade sunk into the armor of its palm and it somehow managed to wrench the sword from her grasp. Its victory was short lived. Brook's other sword plunged into its throat. She gave the blade a good twist before jerking it free. More mechs had joined the melee and were in the process of frying the only wolf other than herself that remained alive. As the last of Grunt's boys went down, Brook knew she was dead. She hoped Brian and Daniel had fared better as more mechs moved to encircle her. She placed both hands on the hilt of her remaining sword and faced them with a loud, roaring growl before their flames enveloped her.

* * *

As Brook died, several blocks away, a cloud of darkness fell over the squads of mechs who guarded the entrance to the giant, black structure that would soon mean the end of life on Earth. From it, Zed led the charge as dozens of human soldiers ran forth from it to engage the mechs. Zed's customized revolvers dropped two with shots to their face-plates before the aliens even fully realized what was happening. Several more of the mechs fell from direct RPG hits and the concentrated fire of the men Zed had led. But the tide of the battle turned the moment the mechs recovered enough to return fire. Soldiers died, crying out, as alien tribarrels mowed them down, bullets pulping their unarmored flesh in explosions of blood and bone fragments. Zed didn't have time to feel bad for leading his men into such a hopeless massacre; it was all he could do to move fast enough to avoid being hit himself. He wove through the streams of rounds that came his way, sidestepping some, ducking others, his revolvers booming. Three more mechs toppled, yellow-edged holes in their faceplates. His plan had driven the aliens into a state of alarm and called away a good portion of their forces from the structure, but not nearly the amount needed for him and his men to have a chance. They weren't going to be able to break through and get inside the thing. All hope now rested with Simon, Kyle, and Grunt. Zed sent a Mech to Hell with a quick, well-placed shot, then he was gone, sprinting away into the city like a bolt of lightning. Behind him, the bodies of his men filled the street at the structure's entrance.

* * *

Simon tossed his small knife aside, trying to appear innocent as two mechs led by one of the aliens entered the holding cell. It was the first time Simon had laid eyes on an alien outside of its armor. The thing didn't have legs in the human sense. It stood and moved about on three tentacle-like limbs that connected to the lower part of its body. A singular arm, ending in three clawed fingers, protruded from each of its sides and its head was triangle shaped, coming to a point where a man's nose would be. On each side of the head were two large eyes. The alien's mouth was on the underside of the triangle's tip. Rows of razor-like teeth glistened inside it, underneath thick, leathery lips. One of its hands held the device Kyle had described to him earlier, and in the other a small disc that it raised to its mouth as it spoke. The disc was some sort of translator; the alien's words came out in English. "Four more are required for the feeding," it told them. "Said number must step forward or *we* will choose who shall receive this honor for you."

"How are you able to know our language?" Kyle asked. The alien slithered around quickly to face the vampire as Simon watched.

"You are a brave one. You may be one of the four."

"You didn't answer me," Kyle pressed. "How did you know of our world?"

The two mechs at the alien's side raised their weapon hands at Kyle but the alien motioned them back. "We have been here before. Not this timeline. Not this world. . . But another that was both this place and not."

"Another timeline? You travel through time?" Kyle stared at the alien, cold and unmoving.

"Our means of transport is of no concern. Choose three more for the feeding," it ordered him.

Kyle shrugged and gestured at Grunt, Simon, and a dark-haired human woman.

"Good," the alien hissed. "Now you come."

"No," Kyle told it, "I don't think so."

Kyle sprang forward, grabbing one the mechs' heads and squashed it between his hands. Grunt moved on the other. The Alpha of the Changed wasn't nearly as strong as the vampire so he tackled the other mech, taking it to the floor of the cell under him as thick, coarse hair grew on his flesh and his expanding muscles ripped his clothes.

"No!" the alien screeched, its translator pressed to its lips. "You must stop this!"

Before it could say more, Simon's claws grew from the tips of his fingers and he tore out its throat. The translator disc fell at its feet as Simon continued to claw away its flesh. Grunt caved in the faceplate of the mech he wrestled with, holding the mech down by its shoulders as he rammed his forehead forward. A throbbing alarm that sounded like a choking cat was blaring.

"What about them?" Simon waved at the humans in the cell with them.

"They're on their own!" Kyle yelled, diving through the doorway of the cell as the membrane there began to reform. "Come on!"

Simon and Grunt followed him into the corridor but none of the humans made it out.

"We'll be back for you," Simon lied, shouting over his shoulder at the men and women in the cell as he ran.

Mechs lumbered into place at both ends of the corridor, trapping the wolves and the vampire between their positions.

"Now what?" Simon asked.

Kyle gave him a sad, half smile. "I suppose it's now or never."

"What?" Simon shouted at him as he realized what Kyle intended to do. "No!"

Then there was only light and heat followed by darkness as the bomb in Kyle's stomach detonated.

* * *

Mordred waited atop the roof of a skyscraper facing the giant, alien structure. He watched as a ball of flame and shrapnel blossomed on its surface. Though from the distance at which he watched it appeared small, he knew it was not. It was wide enough for him to shadow-walk into and he did so. The sky above him became a dark, rough ceiling charred by the explosion as he moved without moving. Now inside the structure, he paused to glance at the area around him. The explosion had done a great deal of damage from the look of things but not nearly as much as the one that was going to follow it would do. He sat the twin nukes contained in his cloak onto the floor and activated them.

"Mordred!" a pained voice called to him. It belonged to Kyle. A small part of the vampire's body with his head and half an arm still attached lay a few feet away. Kyle's flesh was mostly melted away, sloughing off him in chunks, but the vampire still lived. "Help me!" Kyle begged.

"The others?" Mordred asked.

"Dea. . ." was all Kyle managed before his tongue slipped from his mouth to the floor. It landed there with a wet thump. Mordred nodded. He accepted the loss of his brother stoically and scooped up what remained of Kyle as the timers of the nukes ticked down. Shadows rose and embraced him, carrying himself and the vampire away. For a time, they simply ceased to be, becoming one with the darkness. Mordred's consciousness reached out, searching for his uncle. He felt the force of Zed's speed in use and centered in on it. Mordred appeared holding the chunk of meat that was Kyle in the middle of an alleyway where Zed had just come to a stop. Zed leaned against the wall, coughing and fighting for breath.

"Ain't as young as I once was," Zed grumbled, covered in sweat. It dripped from his hair and stained his clothes. "Simon?" he asked as he looked up at Mordred.

Mordred shook his head. He saw Zed glance at the mess that was Kyle. "Can't believe *you* survived."

"We have only minutes, uncle. We must find the others and a ship in which to depart."

"I hear ya," Zed frowned. "You be ready and stay focused on me with. . .with whatever it is you do."

The wind of Zed's departure whipped at Mordred's cloak as the old wolf darted away at a speed of several hundred miles per hour.

* * *

Brian flung three mechs into the ranks of those behind them with the strength of his mind. Nearly three dozen unmoving and broken mechs littered the street around him. Daniel crouched in the partial cover of an apartment building's doorway. Brian stood in the middle of the road between the rows of buildings, holding his own against dozens of mechs who still sought his blood. Tribarrel rounds bounced harmlessly from the telekinetic shield he had erected over his body as he lashed out again, popping the heads of several aliens inside their armored suits. Brian's strength was ebbing with each passing second but he couldn't stop or lower his shield. His family was counting on him and with what the mechs had done to the world, they were all he had left. The comm piece in his ear activated.

"Brian! Brian are you there?" Jennifer's voice crackled over its open channel.

He took hold of one of the mechs' fuel cells and fractured it with his mind. The mech exploded, wounding several others around it. Brian was so exhausted, it pained him to answer his sister.

"Little busy, Jen," he grunted.

"Zed is looking for you. It's time to go!" Jennifer told him. "Can you tell me where you are?"

"No!" he screamed as twin rockets launched from a mech's shoulders burst against his shield and nearly collapsed it. His head stung with blinding pain but he kept the shield up.

"It's okay," Jennifer said. "I'll trace your signal. You just hold on!"

"Doing my best, sis!" He gritted his teeth and slapped his hands together in front of him to help focus his power into a shockwave of force that tore through the mechs, knocking them all from their feet and sending the closer ones flying to bounce along the road. Then suddenly, Zed was there.

"Good job, kid!" Zed smiled at him. "Mordred!" Zed yelled. "Now!"

"Daniel gave up his cover, running to them as Mordred appeared with Kyle in his arms and tendrils of darkness grew, whisking them all away. Brian closed his eyes as his brother's darkness absorbed him. When he opened them, they were standing in a large, wide room that looked to be some kind of hangar bay.

"Out of the frying pan and into the fire. Sorry, kid," Zed said as a section of the room's wall opened like tearing flesh and a group of mechs rushed at them.

* * *

Jennifer rocked back in her chair at the comm station in the mansion war room. An overpowering vision of explosions and death sent shudders through her. She cried out, snapping out of her waking nightmare.

"You okay?" Eyes asked, grabbing her by her arm.

"No," Jennifer answered. "And we're not either."

Eyes looked confused as both of them turned to watch the mushroom cloud rising over New York City on the monitors. The alien structure had been successfully destroyed. Suddenly, the image on the screen became nothing more than static.

"Side effect of the nukes?" Jennifer asked.

"No," Eyes said, her fingers dancing over her keyboard. "The satellite went out of range but at least we know the bombs did their job."

"How can you be sure?"

"How can you see the future?" Eyes shot back at her.

"Oh," Jennifer said, "Duh. I'm sorry."

Eyes nodded at her. "Forget it."

The lights in the war room went out. When they came back online they were dimmer and red. "Oh crap!" Eyes leapt up from her seat. "We've lost power."

"What does that mean?" Jennifer's heart pounded in her chest.

"It means. . ." Eyes drew the pistol on her belt. "Those things have found us."

Eyes yanked Jennifer up. "The soldiers outside will try to fight but this base is lost. We need to leave now."

The whole mansion shook as an explosion boomed somewhere outside. The sound of a tank's main gun answered it as Eyes led Jennifer through the mansion's winding hallways at a full run. Men and women in the uniforms of soldiers and techs rushed by them to help those out-side, but Jennifer knew Eyes had only one goal and that it was to keep the two of them alive. These was a mini airfield for the team's helicopters behind the mansion and both of them were qualified to fly the birds waiting there if the mechs hadn't reduced them to scrap already. They reached a door leading out of the rear of the mansion to the airfield. Eyes threw it open. A mech stood waiting, blocking their path. The last thing Jennifer saw was a wide geyser of fire from its flamethrower erupt-ing towards them before her eyes melted in their sockets.

* * *

Zed's revolvers spat death, dropping mech after mech. Each shot shattering a faceplate and pulping alien flesh underneath. Brian could barely stand. Daniel helped support him while firing his AA-12 one handed. Kyle lay on the floor of the hangar bay, his body trying to regen-erate itself. The vampire had two arms again but his legs were still trying to grow back. Mordred stood over Kyle, casting bolts of shadow at the mechs. The solidified darkness of one bolt pierced a mech's armor like a spear, pinning it to the wall of the bay. He threw a second through the head of another mech, splattering yellow blood.

Daniel's AA-12 clicked empty. "Zed!" he shouted. "Tell me you have a plan!"

Zed reloaded his pistols in a blur, his barrage of fire slowed only by the briefest fraction of a second. "Brian's the plan! He good to go?"

The tide of mechs flooding into the bay continued to grow beyond the group's capacity to handle them. Mordred grunted as he took a trib-arrel burst to his right shoulder. His arm flopped to hang at his side, attached only by thin strands of sinew and meat. Mordred roared, flinging his left hand upwards, erecting a wall of black energy between the group and the mechs.

"Just need a minute," Brian said.

"You don't have it," Mordred growled, beads of sweat and blood dripping from his hair and forehead. "I can't hold them. There's too many."

Zed was so fast Brian didn't even see him move. One second he was at the head of the group near Mordred's barrier, the next his uncle was at his side.

"It's all down to you, boy," Zed told him. "You have got to get to this ship's core and mess it up big time, ya hear?"

Brian nodded.

"Get out of here!" Zed urged him as Mordred screamed in pain and the barrier of black energy collapsed.

Brian focused his will on the far wall of the bay and ripped open a hole that led into a corridor beyond. Daniel had used the short lull

Mordred had created in the battle to reload. "Go!" he shoved Brain at the opening. "We got this!"

Brian jumped through the air, his body changing as he moved. He landed on all fours, covered in fur, and growling in frustration at leaving the others as he ran.

"He's out!" Daniel shouted as he turned to face the mechs again, raising his AA-12. A tribarrel burst tore his chest into a mangled mass of meat and burnt flesh. Daniel fell and moved no more.

"By all that's holy!" Mordred shrieked. "They're using silver now!"

"We all gotta die sometime," Zed laughed as he sped forward into the ranks of the mechs, weaving among them as his revolvers continued to thunder. The old wolf ran up the front of a mech, leaping off its head into another as the streams of tribarrel fire chasing him sent the mech he had jumped from to Hell. The mech he crashed into went skidding across the bay floor with Zed on top of it. He paused long enough to put a point blank shot into its faceplate before moving on.

Mordred created shield after shield, blocking one burst of tribarrel fire then another, trying to hold his ground. "Screw this," the mage yelled and vanished in a puff of shadow.

Zed noticed Kyle was gone as well, though what had happened to the vampire, he had no idea. The entire bay was filled with mechs and Zed had nowhere left to run. He tossed his empty pistols aside and raised his hands over his head as the mechs encircled him.

"On your knees human-thing!" one of the things ordered in a synthesized, robotic voice. "Hands behind your head."

Zed grinned. "I may be old, boys, but I still know how to kick some tail."

The old wolf ripped open his shirt to reveal a mass of explosives strapped around his chest.

"Boom," Zed laughed as the mechs opened fire and the entire bay exploded.

* * *

Brian bounded down the corridor. Startled squid-like creatures flung themselves from his path. He kept on running, ignoring their angry and fear-filled clicks and hisses. His family was dead. His world was in ruins. He rounded a bend in the corridor and wondered where in the Hades he was even headed. Brian had no idea where the core was or how to get to it. He couldn't stop moving though. If he did, the mechs would find him and it would all be over.

"Brian," a cold voice spoke inside his head.

"Kyle?" he thought back at it.

"Yes," the voice answered. "I am here, inside your lungs. I became mist and entered them during the battle."

"That's just gross," Brian replied.

"Nonetheless, I am here with you and I know how to reach the core. Now stop breathing so bloody hard. Do you know how much of me you've breathed out already, despite my efforts to stay inside of you?"

"I can't stop breathing."

"Just slow your breath down. I can do the rest."

Like a professional runner, Brian took control of his panting and slowed it to longer breaths, paced and steady.

"Good," Kyle told him. "That makes it easier."

"The core?" Brian asked, pouring on the speed to slide into a lift with one of the aliens as its membrane door oozed shut behind him. Brian ripped the squid thing apart with his claws as the lift began to descend.

"The core, or engine if you will, is the entire center of the ship, stretching from its top to its bottom with vents that open into space at both ends. I won't pretend to understand the technology. I don't. However, Mordred seemed to, at least to a degree. He thought that if it could be disrupted, the core would undergo a chain reaction that would destroy this entire mothership from the inside out."

"Disrupted how?"

"You're a telekinetic. Use your imagination."

Oh, Brian thought.

On the wall of the lift's interior was a position indicator that showed where it was located in relationship to the other parts of the ship. Brian couldn't read the bizarre alien symbols but he could still tell what it was. He thanked God that the core appeared to be close.

"Take the direct route," Kyle's disembodied voice urged.

"How can you see?" Brian asked. "You don't have eyes at the moment."

"I can't. I am tapping into your eyesight through your thoughts," Kyle explained. "As soon as the membrane rolls back into the wall and this stops, punch it hardcore with all the speed you've got. You are only going to have one shot at this, Brian."

The lift stopped moving and the membrane door melted away. A group of surprised aliens hissed loudly as Brian plunged through them. The pads of his paws smashed against the organic metal floor of the ship as he gave it everything he had. Zed would have been proud of the speed he managed as he rushed passed the aliens towards a massive set of locked down, bulkhead doors. They appeared to be real doors composed of the same black metal as the hulls of the alien dropships instead of membranes like the one on the lift. He figured that meant he was in the right place. There was a mech standing on each side of the doorway, guarding it. They raised their tribarrels at him. As Brian breathed out, a stream of mist, like dragon's breath, emerged from his mouth and nose. Brian zigged and zagged dodging the mechs' first bursts as the mist became solid.

Kyle grabbed each of the mechs by an arm and smashed them together like two colliding cars. Their broken remains clattered to the floor at the vampire's feet. Brian shifted into human form as he drew closer to where Kyle stood.

"Thanks," Brian said.

"The door," Kyle ordered him.

Brian focused his power. As he did so the massive doors shook, thudding back and forth in their frame.

"We've got more company," Kyle warned as five mechs stepped from the lift behind them.

"No, we don't," Brian said in a strained voice. The massive doors tore free of the wall, spinning into the mechs, crushing them under its weight.

The doorway opened into space, a blinding beam of energy the size of an eighteen wheeler reached as far as Brian could see both up and down the length of the shaft. Whistling air rushed out into the void of space, threatening to drag himself and Kyle with it. Brian held himself in place with his power, a field of blue energy encasing his body. Kyle was hurled forward towards the shaft but the vampire caught a hold on the metal of the doorway at the last instance, his pale fingers digging into it.

"The beam, Brian!" Kyle yelled with both his real voice and inside Brian's mind.

Four more mechs, held to the floor of the corridor by magnetic boots, clomped towards them. The lights in the corridor flickered out one by one behind the mechs until they were engulfed in shadow. Mordred was there among them. Both the mechs and Mordred vanished. Only Mordred reappeared. His cloak flopped about him as he held his ground. The mage raised a hand and sealed the hole leading into space around the core with a thin layer of solid darkness. The brightness of the core could still be seen through the barrier. Mordred walked to stand beside Brian.

"Do your job, little brother."

"Little?" Brian smiled.

Mordred glared at him and nodded at the energy beam. Kyle stood with them, waiting.

Brian imagined a disc of pure telekinetic power in the middle of the beam and tried to will it into existence. It formed only to be immediately destroyed. Brian tried again, sinking to his knees from the strain. The pain was blinding but he created the disc and held it against the energy crackling, trying to break through it from both sides. Blood leaked from his eyes and ears but still he held the disc together. The beam of energy parted, moving up and down the length of the shaft away from the disc, blossoming outward into the ship as it went.

"Now!" Kyle shouted at Mordred. "Get us the Hell out of here!"

Mordred, Kyle, and Brian were whisked away by the shadows of the corridor. When the darkness released them, they stood on a hilltop, under a night sky. Rain fell against their skin and a gentle breeze blew through the trees surrounding them.

"Look!" Mordred pointed at the sky above. A massive ball of fire filled the heavens, a rippling explosion of yellow and orange. The ball of fire exploded again, doubling in size, then began to fade away. Smaller bits of fire fell among the clouds like shooting stars.

"We did it," Kyle said.

"That we did," Mordred agreed, "but the war is far from over. There are still many divisions of mechs on Earth that must be dealt with."

Brian wiped tears of blood from his cheeks. "We'll deal with them," he said firmly. "Zed and the others *will* be avenged."

Mordred stared at him. "I figured you would be going home now. You've done all you need to. We can handle things from here."

"No," Brian said. "I'm not going anywhere."

Kyle laughed. "Well then, welcome to the pack."

AUTHOR BIOGRAPHY

ERIC S. BROWN IS KNOWN FOR WRITING SCIENCE FIC-
tion and horror. He has written nearly forty (40) books, most of
them published by Severed Press. He began his writing career
with short "zombie" horror stories, and then wrote his first full-length
novel in 2003, entitled "Dying Days" which was followed by the "Queen"
series, and then "Cowboys vs. Zombies". He now writes creature novels,
post-apocalyptic fiction, and space-marine novels.

Brown began his professional writing career by penning short horror
stories as well as illustrated graphic novels, which began with his first
2003 novel, "Dying Days." In 2004, he co-authored a novel entitled "Por-
tals of Terror" along with Angeline Hawkes Craig.

In 2005, his net novel, entitled "Cobble" was released. It was co-authored by Susan Brydenbaugh Brown and continued with "The Queen"
which dealt with zombies controlling a cruise ship. Next was "Barren
Earth," which was released in 2009. Also released in 2009 was his novel
entitled "World War of the Dead".

After releasing a novel entitled "The Human Experiment," he got his
big break when "Bigfoot War" was released. It was followed by "Dead in
the Woods," which came out in 2011, along with the third entry, "Food
Chain". Along with this new series, Brown wrote and published "The
Bloody Rage of Bigfoot" in 2012.

After writing over six more entries into the Bigfoot War series, Brown
published his first stand-alone novel entitled "Kaiju Dawn" in 2014, which
began another series. Its sequel, "Kaiju Armageddon," was released a few
months later. He wrote seven more entries into the Kaiju series before
publishing his next stand-alone novel, "Megalodon" which was released
on e-book and paperback in April 2015. The next novel he wrote, which
was also released in 2015, was entitled "Megalodons," and was co-authored by Clarence Writz.

His next novel was "Megalodon Apocalypse". Then, in February 2016,
he released a new novel entitled "Kraken," which followed a Navy ship
as it battled horrifying mutant squids. It had good reviews from critics
and customers alike. It was followed by "Alien Battleton," which told the
story of Alien warfare. Then, "Kraken Island" was released just a month
and a half later. It was followed by "Kraken Vs. Megalodon," where Eric
combined the two mighty beasts of the deep.

Copper Dog Publishing LLC

OUR IMPRINTS

Pumpkin Hill Press

To find out more about our imprints
and our upcoming releases, visit our website:
www.CopperDogPublishing.com
or our Facebook page:
www.facebook.com/copperdogpublishing

www.ingramcontent.com/pod-product-compliance
Lightning Source LLC
Chambersburg PA
CBHW060750180626
46818CB00002B/528